Love in the Dunes

Love in the Dunes
Las Vegas Writers on Passion and Heartache

Volume 12

Edited by Jarret Keene

HUNTINGTON PRESS
LAS VEGAS, NEVADA

Love in the Dunes
Las Vegas Writers on Passion and Heartache
Volume 12

Published by
Huntington Press
3665 Procyon Street
Las Vegas, NV 89103
Phone (702) 252-0655
e-mail: books@huntingtonpress.com

Edited by: Jarret Keene

Contributing Writers: Emily Bordelove, Melissa Bowles-Terry, Bob Dancer, Kimberley Idol, Jarret Keene, Heather Lang-Cassera, Nicole Minton, Jen Nails, Krystal Ramirez, Brett Riley, Nicholas Russell, Tonya Todd, Mauricio Ortiz Zaragoza

ISBN: 978-1-944877-50-7
$13.95us

Cover Artist: Shan Michael Evans
Cover Design: Christopher Smith
Production & Design: Alison Holka

Las Vegas Writes 2021 is supported by public and private funding for the literary arts through Nevada Humanities, the National Endowment for the Humanities, the Nevada Center for the Book, Nevada State Library Archives and Public Records, Institute of Museum and Library Services, the Las Vegas-Clark County Library District, Las Vegas-Clark County Library District Foundation, and Huntington Press. The program receives additional support, with readings and conversations hosted at venues that support the literary arts, from the City of Las Vegas Office of Cultural Affairs, The Writer's Block Bookstore, and the 2021 Las Vegas Book Festival.

www.nevadahumanities.org/project-grants

Contents

Contents

Introduction:
The Heart Wants What It Wants

By Jarret Keene

Last year was challenging on so many fronts that only one theme seemed obvious and necessary for the 2021 edition of Las Vegas Writes. After all, nothing cures the anguish of life like love. Maya Angelou, in one of her beautiful memoirs, expressed it best when she wrote, "Love heals. Heals and liberates." She describes love as "a condition so strong that it may be that which holds the stars in their heavenly positions." Sure, scientists today credit dark matter as the mysterious glue holding together the universe. But what if Angelou is correct by suggesting that deep affection, that intense pleasure generated by our adoration for another, is what actually keeps galaxies intact? Or the tenderness of God perhaps? The intimacy of a benevolent computer intelligence responsible for this beautiful simulation that we inhabit? Indeed, when I was younger, I used to believe in theories derived from scientific calculations and observations. The older I get, the more I sense another force pushing the world forward, spinning perfectly on its axis. Today, I discern a metaphysical explanation for our existence—and for our finding reasons to exist—on a planet that can often wound us terrifically before destroying us completely.

And so love presented itself, ripe for exploration, ready for celebration. There was a rub, of course: As we all suspect and have confirmed with our own lived experiences, any power that restores our spirits can also gouge our hearts. Very often we find ourselves nicked by love's double edge. Desire, for example, complicates our intentions and muddies the clear waters of romance with the ichor of lust, the spillage of savage craving. Of course, romance fiction, that much-maligned category of literary production, has long basked in the tension between the heart and eroticism. But not all of us manage to balance the two so expertly. Sometimes we allow one side or the other to overwhelm us, to get the better of us, to push us to our breaking points. The trickiness of love—the huge risk and spectacular reward that go along with securing our beloved—accounts for why Las Vegas is now the hottest post-pandemic travel destination, especially as the miserable loneliness of 2020 recedes in the rearview. People are eager to take another chance on love, to roll the dice of sensual hunger on the crap table of human need. They want to gamble for the highest stakes imaginable, pushing nothing less than themselves—their bodies and hearts—into the figurative pile of poker chips, hoping for a royal flush.

And who can explain why they—why we—do it? As the poet Emily Dickinson wrote to a friend, "The heart wants what it wants," and there is no easy way to explain passion. We can only feel it and feel for those of us caught up in its maelstrom before we soar, then crash and burn.

Despite enduring the moniker "Sin City" due to its abundant vice offerings, Las Vegas is, in its own way, a town of devotion and commitment. On average, 300 couples every 24 hours tie the knot in this disreputable city, swamping the Clark County Marriage License Bureau—open until midnight daily and located in the Regional Justice Center, in the same edifice where judges sentence criminals to prison for domestic abuse and spousal murder. Drive along Lewis Street downtown after sunset and you will undoubtedly contemplate how strong the feelings of love must be as you observe hordes of people filling out paperwork on the hoods of their Uber rides by phonelight, all for the purpose of then undergoing a drive-thru wedding ceremony that lasts, at most, a few minutes. Las Vegas is where love is defined and enshrined, where romance blossoms like bright flowers in a beige-mazed desert. For a place infamous for depravity, the city offers thousands a chance at old-fashioned nuptial bliss.

Even the most lurid nooks of Las Vegas display, to a small degree, sentimentality and fondness. Think about it: How many tech-sector men have arrived here in paper-thin sweatpants to enjoy a lap dance, only to fall in love with a stripper, promising to rescue her from her debauched lifestyle and set her up in a Silicon Valley apartment? How many women have shown up for a night of honky-tonk line dancing with gal-friends, only to swoon mightily to a few lines from a Podunk hunk and then ditch the crew for an extended week of passion in a Boulder Highway RV park? You might insist these are clichés and none of these things actually happen. Well, after 20 years of living here, I've witnessed them firsthand. It's all fun and games—until someone surrenders their heart.

No one knows this like a Las Vegas writer. As the authors selected for this volume began to send me their short stories, I found myself awash in the blood and guts of love, horrified and thrilled by what I was reading. I confess that I had anticipated a collection of fiction that was, on the whole, light, humorous, even superficial. After all, love is—if the thousands of insubstantial Hollywood rom-coms are any indication—a subject that lends itself to diaphanous treatment and Hallmark-style kitsch. Instead, these stories went marrow-deep in answering the question: How does one find (and frequently lose) love in a valley of controlled avarice and aphrodisia?

The answers are varied and fascinating. In this book, twelfth in the Las Vegas Writes series and the second I have edited for Nevada Humanities, you will discover writers wrestling with the thorny issue of love and passion, infatuation and heartbreak, commitment and infidelity in never-before-expressed ways. From Melissa Bowles-Terry's bittersweet tale of a Sapphic fling between two ambitious college librarians who can't quite get on the same page and Kimberley Idol's devastating chronicle of a doomed marriage of literary writers fraught with dire symbolism and foreshadowing (all of it ignored and excused) to Nicole Minton's acidic and agonizing peek into the world of "sugaring," a transactional relationship in which a younger woman is financially cared for by an older, wealthier man, this collection of short fiction illuminates the goriest contours of dysfunctional yearning.

To my (and I hope your) utter delight, a few of the stories gathered here are straight-up genre, including Emily Bordelove's werewolf hockey player-meets-witch grad student rescue that pits the couple in question against a vampire horde responsible for kidnapping the werewolf's sister. Nicholas Russell, meanwhile, presents what has to be the most thought-provoking piece of pure Las Vegas science-fiction I've read in years in the form of a time-travel saga in which the manager of a chronometric entertainment facility in Sin City observes his beloved appear and disappear and reappear at different points in her life, while knowing full well that at some point in the not-so-distant past/present/future they will be together. And for those readers who relish the grungier "post-apocalyptic adventure" category, poet Heather Lang-Cassera shows off her narrative chops with a haunting mother-daughter yarn that boasts ear-drum-deafening whales in the sky, somnambulation, and a new appreciation for madrigal music that will take your breath away and leave you in stunned silence.

There is a selection of experimental fiction, too, that will impress the most jaded literary connoisseur. Jen Nails's lyric narrator introduces us to three different types of Las Vegas-based love stories set in different locales, weaving poetry before, after, and within each blossoming relationship in a Walt Whitman-on-ecstasy style that you have to read yourself to fully grasp. Tonya Todd tests the limits of anticipation with delightful results in her build-up to a young woman's bet with her best friend that will either prove her right (that her heart is permanently closed) or that will prove her bestie correct (that she is only one date away from finding love). Then there is Las Vegas artist Krystal Ramirez, who gives us a series of text-based works that cause us to reconsider what we think about when we visually absorb (rather than intellectually analyze) the language—words and their associations—of romance.

Finally, there is also plenty of gritty fiction that Las Vegas authors are known for producing, including Mauricio Ortiz Zaragoza's brutal story of a graveyard-shift custodian who can clean up everything save the mess of relationships that surround him and threaten to engulf his parents. Bob Dancer, a video poker expert who has written several books on the subject, takes us on a tour of a Mother's Day casino tournament in which the narrator's mother-in-law runs off with more than the prize money. Brett Riley, a college professor and writer of Western murder-mysteries, shows us that casino security jobs can offer an eye-level perspective on the promise of love, even when the oath sworn is more than a few decades old.

The stories in this book capture the fullest range of sudden affection and shattering loss, all of it occurring under the neon glare and in the sandy, windswept dunes of the valley. I am so happy to be sharing these fictions with readers hungry for something different, something thoughtful and palpable. I am so grateful for the writers gathered here, for their sensitive approaches to the difficult task of giving voice to emotions that we all too often take for granted or obscure for our own protection. I credit them—along with Huntington Press, artist Shan Michael Evans, designer Christopher Smith, and Nevada Humanities Program Manager Bobbie Ann Howell—for constructing this gorgeous book that you now hold in your hands.

The Canyon I Never Reached

By Melissa Bowles-Terry

It was the first day of fall semester and I was starting grad school. I found myself in the same town, with
the same roommates in the same off-campus house,
walking across the same quad where I'd spent the last
four years. A combination of nerves, lack of funds, and
a family crisis had conspired to immobilize me, keeping
me at this agricultural college where I'd just completed
my bachelor's degree three months prior.

I trudged up to the run-down English building on the
corner of the quad. For decades, no one had cared
that it was overrun with box-elder bugs, the carpet in
the basement smelled, or that the concrete of the front
steps was crumbling. Today a new girl sat on those

crumbling stairs. She had a small circle gathered around her, where she sat with very long, tan legs folded under her. As I walked toward the circle I saw my friend Katie, the only other new grad student I knew from our recent life as undergraduates, and we skirted the new kids and walked in together to begin learning about our responsibilities as graduate instructors, teaching first-year students the mysteries of academic writing.

On the second day of our orientation I walked into the ladies' room in the English building and found the long-legged new girl looking in the mirror, skirt hiked up, checking the tattoo on her hip that was still healing.

"Oh, hi," I said, startled by the view, but trying to play it cool. "That looks amazing." Actually, it was cheesy and looked painful, a dragon circling her muscular runner's thigh.

She sighed. "It's not what I had pictured. It never is, you know?"

And then she walked out.

I later learned her name was Amanda. I already had my circle of friends in town, plus a boyfriend, and I wasn't really looking to branch out. And this girl, Amanda, was one of the cool kids, organizing the new graduate students for dinner parties and bonfires. I kept her and the other grad students at a distance. When I finally had a real conversation with Amanda, after I observed her teaching her first-year English class, I learned that before graduate school she'd taught high school in Las Vegas for five years. She knew what she was doing in the class-room, unlike the rest of us who bumbled along with students who were more like peers. I admired her confidence and was in awe of the way she commanded students' respect while wearing weird thrift-store clothes and rainbow hair. I confessed to her that I wasn't sure I had anything useful to teach first-year students about writing, and she cocked her head: "You know more than *they* do. Just remember that."

At the end of our first year, Amanda and I were assigned a special project. We'd spend the summer together, revising the first-year writing course. I agreed to do it because I needed the money. I wasn't sure why *she* wanted to, but I was relieved to be partnered with someone who knew what they were doing. Every day in May we were shut up in a little office in the English department, planning reading and writing assignments. We started hanging out at night, too, watching *Project Runway* and *Sex in the City*. We took ourselves out to dinner, drove up the canyon. It turned flirty when she told me that I reminded her of her best friend in high school.

"She was a cute little blonde girl, just like you," she said. "And she knew exactly how to use her cute-little-blonde-girl power, just like you, to get what she wanted."

I was flustered when Amanda flirted with me, but pleased. She was the most interesting-looking person I'd ever met, which sounds like faint praise, but it's not. Looking back at photos, I can barely tell that she's gorgeous. She's always making a stupid face.

One of our professors explained it perfectly, if inappropriately. At a department party, gesturing with her glass of wine, she was talking about Amanda. "You know how little girls don't care if they're showing their underwear? They just run wild, doing cartwheels? Well, one day we all became painfully aware of what we were doing and started sitting with our legs together. But not Amanda."

In June I took off for a week to go to a family reunion in Idaho. Amanda texted me every day, and I sent little anecdotes that I thought would entertain her.

-*My cousin brought a classic Jell-O salad [pic]*

-*My grandma wants to know why I didn't bring my boyfriend, and why he hasn't proposed yet [shrug emoji]*

-*Brothers won't stopping talking about a batch of semen that went bad before they could inseminate the heifers [barf emoji]*

I got back and she told me she couldn't wait to go to my next family reunion with me to see rural life up close for herself.

"City girl," I laughed at her. "Didn't inseminate many heifers in Vegas, did you?"

We went to an academic conference in L.A. and did the whole thing super-cheap. Amanda had friends who knew people—an actor who'd been on a police show and a writer who'd worked on a sitcom. We ended up staying with her friends, going to hot bars and a house party in Silver Lake. At the party a writer, Becky, was flirting hard with me and I kept looking over at Amanda to see if she had noticed. She did.

We kissed for the first time that night. Not at the bar and not at the party, but back in the bedroom we were sharing, sleeping on the floor. First we were spooning and her breath on my neck was boozy and sweet when she asked, "Do you like Becky? Is she your type?"

"I think she's cute."

"Have you been with a woman before?"

"No, never. Have you?"

"My first time was with one of my professors at UNLV. It was in her office and I was . . . surprised."

Then, jealous of that unnamed old lady professor, I rolled over to face Amanda and she kissed me.

It didn't change things at first. We went back to the university to finish revising that first-year writing curriculum. I took Amanda with me to my grandmother's house for a 4th of July breakfast, and her cupcake-pink hair and mile-long legs made my uncles look twice, but everyone was perfectly well behaved. Amanda asked my grandfather, a retired farmer, how he kept his flower-beds so colorful in the middle of the hot summer, and he was delighted to share his secret watering and fertilizing schedule.

Then, suddenly, summer was winding down. One night we were riding our bikes down the canyon road and she proposed a backpacking trip. "We have to do it before the semester starts. You're going to love Havasupai so much! It's the most beautiful waterfall in the world." It sounded like hell to me, carrying all my gear and sleeping on the ground, but I'd suffer more than that for the chance to spend a week with her. Better yet, the drive to the trailhead would take us straight through her hometown of Las Vegas. I was dying to see her in the place she was from, to see if it made her make sense, the way I felt most logical and peaceful when I was in Idaho.

I started rounding up some gear. Borrowed a back-pack from a friend. Bought hiking boots and wore them everywhere for a week to break them in. Bought dried food and water-purifying tablets. We started early in the morning and drove all day, straight down through Utah and into Las Vegas. Amanda's parents were on a church-mission trip in Brazil and had been away from the family home for months. Her brother lived down the street and had been keeping an eye on things. We walked into this little ranch house and it was so hot and stuffy, with mauve wall-to-wall carpet in the family room. One wall was covered with big senior portraits of Amanda and her four siblings. I walked over to the wall to inspect. She was obviously the pretty one.

"Want to take a shower?" she asked me. We had been in the car all day. We hopped in the shower together, giggling and soaping each other up. It was more playful than steamy, then we put on fresh T-shirts and underwear and watched *Notting Hill* in her parents' bed. Next day we stopped for breakfast at a burrito place that had been haunting Amanda's dreams ever since she left town, and we finished our drive to Havasupai.

We got out of her little blue sedan, sat in the open trunk, and pulled on our hiking boots. This was it. It was noon and we needed to hike 10 miles down into the canyon and set up camp. As we hiked down and down and down, I thought there wasn't much to see. I didn't have any experience with desert hiking; my Idaho-mountain upbringing suggested that a hike was breathing in pine trees and going to the top of a mountain. This felt backwards, starting at the top and hiking down into a canyon. And there were certainly no pine trees. Amanda pointed out barrel cactus, Mormon tea, creosote, and mesquite. It all looked muted to me, shades of brown. Ugly terrain. She laughed at me, "What, you want to hike barefoot in the moss like a little forest fairy? Desert hiking makes you tough!"

My backpack was heavy on my shoulders. The friend it belonged to was three inches taller than me, so the bottom of the backpack was bumping along on my butt instead of at my waist. The fronts of my thighs were burning with the constant *down, down, down* of this trail, and the heat was intense. Amanda was a high school and college track star, had legs that went on forever, and ADHD energy that never stopped. I was doing my best to keep up with her. We hiked all afternoon and when the long summer day was almost over we came to the falls. I couldn't believe the color. I'd never seen anything like it. We set up camp and could hear the falls from where we slept.

At the midpoint of our backpacking trip, Amanda wanted to do a day hike into the Grand Canyon. We'd rested for three days, eating our freeze-dried food, purifying water from the river, sleeping under the stars, and felt ready for a challenge. We climbed down rock walls and crossed a stream, and hiked along for a few miles. Then we came to the spot where we'd have to cross the river. It involved climbing a rope and swinging across.

I doubted my upper-body strength. I was afraid of the river taking me away. My insides were screaming, *This is not OK!*

Amanda was already climbing the rope.

I shouted, "Amanda? I don't think I can do this. This isn't for me."

"Of course you can! It's fine!"

"No, I'm going back to camp."

"Are you kidding me? We're halfway there!"

I turned around and walked back to camp. Amanda went on by herself.

I lay on my sleeping bag and read a book. I bathed and shaved my armpits in the river. I ate tuna fish from a pouch and dreamed about another burrito. When she finally came back, Amanda told me what I'd missed.

"It was incredible," she said. "I was right at the bottom of the canyon, looking up at the face of it."

I smiled and listened. We spent one more day in camp, then hiked back up out of the canyon and drove back to our real lives.

As the summer ended, we were both deep in thesis research and making plans for the following year. She was writing a thesis about Tupac Shakur and planning to go to University of Washington for a PhD. I was writing about the poet Marianne Moore and applying to library and information-science programs. It seemed that, having finished our joint project, we were drifting apart. I started spending more and more time with my boyfriend. She went back to her grad-school crew.

Mid-year, she got accepted to UW and went to Seattle for a visit. Afterwards she came over to my house, unannounced. She presented me with a small gift bag. I pulled out a lavender mug that said *udub girls have more fun.*

"University of Washington has one of the top library-science programs in the country," she said. "And Seattle is so beautiful. You could go with me. We could do the next chapter together."

I wanted to go, but I couldn't find the guts. "You know, my boyfriend Tyler finally proposed. We're talking about moving to Illinois for library school."

She was already walking away. "OK, well, just let me know if you change your mind."

She slammed her car door.

Years later I found myself living in Las Vegas with my husband and toddler, falling deeply in love with the city and the beautiful desert. But an opportunity came up for a job interview in Seattle. Amanda and I had only been in occasional contact, birthday presents and Christmas cards sent through the mail. I texted Amanda to tell her I was coming to town and she invited me to dinner and to join her for a book-group meeting. I read the novel on the plane, *The Children of Men* by P.D. James. The book was published in 1992, but set in England in 2021. The book was 25 years old by that time, and I had no idea why they were reading it. Was it a dystopian book club?

It was a mediocre novel.

We met at a chic downtown place with a dozen tables inside. She wasn't bleaching her hair and dying it rainbow colors anymore, and it was a beautiful rich chestnut that I'd never seen. I got out of my little rental car and she ran up to me in the parking lot and squeezed me.

"God, you feel good," I couldn't help but say.

"You look good enough to eat!" she replied.

Book group was some tech developers, some University of Washington grad students, some teachers from the high school where Amanda taught English.

We discussed: What is the infertility in the book really *about?*

Back at my hotel's bar, just the two of us, she asked me about the job interview and I tried to blow it off.

"I'm just here to test the waters, stay sharp, make sure I've still got it," I winked. "I don't think I'm the right fit for the job anyway."

"So you're not serious about moving to Seattle. You're just stringing them along? Because I know Dr. Allen. He's on that search committee. I'll talk to him. You could move here!"

She was getting too excited. "Amanda, no. You don't need to talk to him."

"You're saying you won't take the job?" She was pissed.

"No, I will. I mean, I *would* take it if they offered it. I want to be with you again."

"What about your boyf—husband? Would he come along?"

"Yes, of course. We have an amazing life together. You need to meet our son!"

"What about me?" she asked flatly.

I kissed her. "I love you! It'll be just like it was before."

At breakfast the next morning Amanda was jumpy, kept getting up for more jam for her toast, tracking down almond milk for her coffee. I rubbed her shoulder and thigh, but everything was tensed and ready for flight.

I dropped Amanda off at her quiet, clean house with a quick goodbye and drove slowly to a silent conference room at the university where I paced and prepared for my job talk. Could I move now? The moment for Seattle, for Amanda and me, had passed. But I nailed the interview and made everyone on the committee smile and laugh and fall in love with me. I was the perfect candidate for them, and I knew it. When I got the job offer a few weeks later, I didn't have to think about it.

"I'm staying where I am," I said to the department chair. "Thank you, though. For the opportunity."

Amanda never replied to the text in which I made excuses for my decision. I explained myself poorly. I was never good at that part.

Whenever I'm hiking outside Las Vegas these days, which is often, I think about her. Her hands felt like desert sand had smoothed them. Her eyes were the pale blue of a blazing August day.

She's the sliding door I didn't make it through, the path I didn't choose, the canyon I never reached.

I chose the life I built in the desert instead of the girl who loved it.

It's not what I pictured. But it never is, you know?

Weeds in the Garden

By Kimberley Idol

In her mind Las Vegas was a place for strangers to meet. A transitional place, not somewhere you put down roots or made permanent commitments. Las Vegas shouldn't exist. A gangster's daydream, not a place to live but a place to pass through and escape in time. Las Vegas was where she met her husband, who confirmed these rules. Her husband thought she'd help him grow and she thought he'd make her feel safe. He made love indifferently, like a man afraid of intimacy, but who understood the need to pretend. It was as if he'd read about love in a manual and knew it was supposed to exist, but didn't want to share the experience with her. For all she knew now, he'd since found it with someone else. Looking back, she could see that his attitude aligned with her philosophy of relationship maintenance. She wouldn't have kids with him, because he was unsuitable for that, so she let that wish go. Sex for him was when he shut down, so she let hope for a healthy sex life go. He'd never pretended to be trustworthy, so she accepted that. Still fighting for a better day, she rejected six marriage proposals, but then she stopped hoping for the kind of marriage in which she mattered. You can get married and divorced in a week in Las Vegas. It's not a place for permanence. She let a lot of ideas slip away into the divide that became their marriage. The purpose of the two of them would be him and discussions about how whatever she wanted interfered with an all-consuming sense of entitlement that made him jealous of her desires. When he did comply with the role of husband, it was as if he'd read a description of one in a textbook and was following that passage very closely, so that he could say that he'd been a good guy.

The first time they had sex was as a threesome and the second time he came too fast. She should have paid attention.

Now, after it was all over, she stood outside in her yard with the divorce decree in one hand and a cup of lukewarm coffee in the other and tried to make sense of the waste. Her yard was full of weeds, but she had always liked weeds. In Las Vegas the weeds blossomed in the fall and the spring in vigorous waves. She thought of them as scruffy inhabitants making the best of a difficult situation when they poked up through the bad soil. She liked the weird plant that pushed through cracks in the patio and grew tiny yellow berries. She loved the messy crush growing in her flowerbeds, the pale green telegraph plant, the spotted spurge that covered the ground like ivy and could be easily pulled up, the purple mallow, and the white bindweed. She admired the willowy mesquites that popped up in between her rose bushes and provided shade if you just let them grow.

When it came time to cull the overgrowth in her yard, she kept some of the weeds because they were pretty and because she wanted to preserve those messy survivalists that she felt had earned the right to succeed. She let them live in between her desert roses, next to the one oak tree, and near the stand of sumac she'd rescued from a weird bug infestation. Now, in the days when she was just barely surviving because the divorce was a killing affair, she also let the weeds stay; she didn't have the heart or the energy to remove them.

They'd been talking but not dating for months before they'd had sex for the first time. He was an emotional mess and while needy men were labor intensive, she felt comfortable around them. They were a responsibility she understood, and dating narcissists meant that she could preserve a certain amount of distance. Narcissists were always paying attention to themselves. She would never have to peer too deeply into her own soul as long as she and her husband were together, because the project of their relationship would always only be him. She'd be too busy. She'd be too tired to think about what she was giving up by marrying a child and staying in Las Vegas because that's where he needed to be.

She was a year ahead of him in an MFA program. At their first meeting he said he'd just divorced his wife and left her behind in Utah.

"For a while it was pretty perfect," he said. "I haven't had to work for the past ten years unless I wanted to."

"How'd you work that out?"

"Disability. I'm a diagnosed schizophrenic. My ex-wife, too. Between the two government checks we could stay high and rent an apartment and have a cat."

"A cat?"

"I left him behind when I left her and she had him killed." She didn't know what to say to that, so she let it go.

"Are you still schizophrenic or whatever?" she asked. They were standing in the campus counseling center waiting to make appointments.

"I don't think so." He shook his head. "But I take lots of

drugs. Xanax, Clozapine, Ativan, Ritalin, Zoloft, anti-depressants, anti-anxiety, anti-psychotics. And I still need prescriptions filled, because you can't just stop taking them."

"You take them all at once?"

"I switch them up," he said. "My mom was worried about me as a teenager. I told her that I could talk to angels and that I was seeing them, so she took me to a doctor and they got me started on the drugs. And I stayed that way. But I've cut back now, because I want to go to school. I want to write poetry."

There it was. The University of Nevada, Las Vegas offered a stipend to anyone who was accepted, and with that money he could afford an apartment and remain unemployed as long as he didn't need much.

"How old are you now?"

"Twenty-seven," he said. Fifteen years younger. "Starting fresh." He had moved to Utah as a teenager, but had grown up in Las Vegas. For him enrolling at UNLV was like coming home. The campus seemed set in the middle of nowhere, surrounded by low-income housing and strip malls. Only a few miles from the Strip, the campus spread a concrete presence that offered no more a sense of community than Las Vegas itself.

They met in the counseling center. He needed a refill for his prescriptions, and she was depressed. He latched onto her, hoping to win for himself some of the strength he saw in her, and she saw an opportunity to build a desert dream around him. She was lonely. Sex clubs were fun, but she wanted someone to come home to and as long as she dated him, he'd keep her busy and keep her company. She'd keep the household bills in her name, because he didn't mind not paying the bills now and then. And as long as that was her job, if he abandoned her, she wouldn't be in too much trouble. She loved her house and she loved the view of the desert and Red Rock Canyon. It offered a calming sense of wilderness that overrode the city's high-life aspect. She would keep all that in her name in case he bolted. But as time passed, and despite herself, she started to trust her husband. There would be good times. Her job as his wife would be to clear the way for him to succeed, to get him sober, to get him to graduate, to help him find a job. As for the qualities he didn't have, that she wanted her man to have, she'd make them up. She wanted a partner. She'd try it this way, try to build one from scratch. Good for him. Good for her.

The first time they had sex wasn't planned. When she looked at the calendar later on, she realized it was on the anniversary of D-Day; an appropriate anniversary, given the way things went.

That first night he was still recovering from a nervous

breakdown. He'd shown up at a friend's apartment three weeks earlier babbling, and they'd taken him in hand and walked him over to the nearest psychiatric facility. She covered his campus tutoring shifts while he was hospitalized. His friends tried to contact his family when he melted down, but they couldn't find his father and his mother had refused to become involved. It wasn't until much later that they all realized his problems were drug-induced as much as anything else. Once released from the hospital he'd gone right back to it. He became cannier about hiding his issues, letting the demons run free in spurts, so that he just looked like another grad student who overindulged from time to time.

He became good friends with a particularly noxious trio of potheads who had shifted into 'shrooms and coke use in the second year of their master's program. They were all keeping their heads above water at school, but every holiday and each weekend they let loose. On Fridays they would collect all the paraphernalia, drugs, food, and drink they needed to make it through to Monday, set up the game center, and invite all who were willing to disembark from Earth for a couple of days. The crowd holed up in the apartment of the one who lived closest to the university.

He had agreed to meet her at the party, but it wasn't a date. The party was a muted bacchanalia. No one was screaming, no one set the furniture on fire or kicked in the TV set. She didn't drink or use drugs, but she enjoyed the company. She also had no idea how involved he was in terms of the drugs. As per her pattern with the men she dated, she wasn't paying attention to the possible pitfalls that everyone else could spot right away. They were reaching the point where not having sex was odd given how close they'd become, but he didn't have the experience and she wanted to be pursued, just once.

She arrived at the party after he did. It was a stripped-down apartment in a student-housing complex, tiled floors, stucco walls, a working air-conditioner and a fridge full of beer. The only piece of furniture in the apartment belonging to the tenant was a universal workout bench. A super skinny dude, he was trying to bulk up.

Passing through the living room, she saw partygoers in small groups huddled around their favorite party favors—coke, pot, 'shrooms, booze, and acid tabs. Everybody nursed a beer. Cases of the stuff were stacked up next to the fridge, because it was filled to the brim and a trashcan was set up in the bathroom for empties. If you wanted to smoke cigarettes you had to go outside. Smokers sat on the walkway while they looked up at the sky, the stars, and the criss-crossing casino skylights.

Aside from the weight bench there was nothing in the apartment that mattered to its inhabitant except for a PlayStation and the headgear and hand controls for gamers who were online playing some version of shoot-to-kill with whomever else was also online at the time. She spotted her guy standing amid a cluster of men snorting coke off the kitchen countertop. Since drugs didn't interest her, she joined the group playing the video games and started heckling the remote team.

She didn't remember afterwards whose idea it was, but at some point during the night, she found herself in bed with a gay guy who wanted to screw the guy she wanted to screw, and the guy she wanted to screw was too high to be useful to either of his sex partners. They left the bedroom door open, not so that people could watch, but because none of them cared what people saw. At one point she looked up to see a friend standing in the doorway smiling at the scene, his eyes so bright they sparkled. As far as the gay guy was concerned, she was in the way, though he didn't mind her participation if her presence got the man he wanted into his bed. Both men were tall and soft-bodied specimens. Her guy was about twenty pounds overweight and very pale with stretch marks on his thighs, stomach, and ass from when he had been fifty pounds heavier. The other one was albino white with an acne flush across his face and chest and he smelled like a locker room. Both men were high, but her guy was flaccid and passive, and everyone should have guessed how the thing was going to play out when he entered the room so dull-eyed. When he undressed and joined his partners, she saw that he had a very short, curved penis and realized that he was going to have to develop some skills in order to make it useful. She and the gay guy got him hard once, but he didn't have the staying power. The three of them played around for a while, but when no one got where they wanted to go, she eventually gave up, got up, and dressed. Her guy passed out and the gay guy sighed, put on some underwear, and plodded back out to the living room to get a beer. She left the party soon after that.

The second time they had sex, she went to his apartment, which was kept in exactly the same state as the skinny guy's place. He didn't have a bed, but he had a mattress. He had no skills and came within minutes, giving her the burden of telling him that she didn't mind and that he would improve over time.

Because he was young, she figured that it was just a matter of proper training. She was wrong there, but since they weren't officially a couple yet, she figured she could keep going to the sex clubs and satisfy her needs while she began a relationship with the guy who didn't know how to screw. He got better in that he learned how to hold on until she came, and because he was new, the novelty helped her get off. She kept thinking he would get better. He didn't like suggestions, but he said stories about her sex life before he came along turned him on, so that helped a bit. Still, he didn't want to try anything new. She took him to a sex club once and while he could get it up, he couldn't finish, so they didn't do that again and she realized that she was going to have to give up the clubs if she wanted the guy. It seemed disloyal to go without him and she was all in in terms of the relationship she dreamed they might have. She was too committed to the idea of the man he could be, the man he said he wanted to be, so reality was already taking second position to her dreams of a relationship. She learned to have a healthy imagination when they screwed. Eventually, she convinced herself that he loved her, so she resigned herself to having a bad sex life as long as they were in love. How long that would last without satisfying sex she didn't know and maybe she should have thought that out.

Sex with her eventual husband was like a long-distance relationship. It was when he was so close that she became more aware of his anger toward her and his disappointment and she recoiled, dove inside herself while she tried to stay present. But the weird rejection he presented whenever they made love killed any affection she had for him. When they were in bed, she needed protection most from the man who didn't want her near, but who also wanted her to satisfy drives he refused to explain. Again, this should have bothered her more, but she didn't want to lose him and was willing to pay any price in order to keep him.

Three weeks later in an awkward exchange, he told her that he loved her. She'd driven him to the bus station and as he got out of the car he tossed out the phrase. She wasn't looking for the traditional romantic moment, but he said, "I love you" as if he was testing the phrase out. She replied that she hoped he had a good winter break and drove off. It wasn't that she didn't care for him, but to have the words tossed at her on the curb didn't sell it.

He went home to his mother's house for winter break and she went to Mexico. She'd booked two weeks at a resort long before they'd met. They talked on the phone while she was there and she told him she'd been over-whelmed by his admission, but that she loved him too and that she was a little scared. He told her they'd be all right and that they'd both have to learn to trust one another, teach each other how to love one another, and work on having better sex. And he did pursue her. It was his idea that they move in together. It was his idea that they marry. She had just enough sense to hold off until he got himself an actual job and committed to a financial plan and a future. The fact that he was still addicted to pills and alcohol, the fact that he wasn't a good guy just didn't matter so much. He'd change. She'd stand by him no matter what and he'd change. But he never stopped being the only thing he cared about and she never stopped hoping despite all the evidence.

Years later, after so much failure, one of the things he complained about was the fact that she didn't seem to enjoy sex and that it seemed unfair to condemn him to that fate. While she stood in her yard looking over the divorce decree, she wondered how long it would take to want to weed the garden again.

D-Day.

She should have paid better attention.

Sugar

By Nicole Minton

The hardest part of finding a new sugar daddy is sorting through all the messages. This was exactly what Sofia found herself doing late Tuesday night, her mind not allowing rest until she found a potential match. Curiosity and insomnia overwhelmed her. Wearing an oversized men's T-shirt with a mug of chamomile in hand, she basked in the glow of her dying laptop, the bedroom's only source of light. It always amazed her how quickly the messages came. Just that morning she had created a new account with another cutesy made-up name, burner email, and fake number from WhatsApp, and less than twelve hours later she had more than fifty men wanting to meet her. No matter what the guy looked like or what career field he was in, every email sounded the same.

Wow, you're very beautiful. I saw your profile and think we'd make a great match. I love helping students. What kind of arrangement are you looking for?

They're always careful with their word choice, omitting anything bordering illegality. If they say "rate," it means they're a cop. Or worse, a scam. Against her better judgment, Sofia once met a guy despite his usage of the red-flag word. She walked into the bar, saw his polyester suit and Velcro wallet, and immediately made a beeline to the exit. Blocking his number on her way back to her little gray Honda, Sofia felt annoyed she had paid for parking for no reason.

The real, experienced guys always use a specific vocabulary. It's always arrangement, gifts, PPM, and allowance. The last one threw Sofia off every time it was used; it made her feel like a kid saving for a toy. Regardless, her price went higher and higher each time the question of gifts was asked. Once, a balding man in his late sixties gave her five hundred just to have lunch with him a few miles outside the Las Vegas Strip. They ate Mexican food in near silence, the man offering little when she tried initiating conversation. He gave her a few hundred again the next day when they met for coffee, even after she revealed she didn't find him to be a good match. He nodded knowingly, like he'd expected Sofia to say it wouldn't work. He casually slid an envelope her way, gently cupped one of her ring-clad hands, and left without another word. She slipped one of many twenties into the tip jar on her way out, two full lattes abandoned on the table. More often than not, this is where meetings led. A rule Sofia had established for herself early on was that she wouldn't enter into a sugar relationship unless she actually liked the guy. She may not have always been physically attracted to the men she met, but at least she would enjoy their company.

Sofia had been in a handful of these relationships, the first when she was nineteen. She didn't know about the websites or apps for arrangements just yet and was weary of the men who approached her. Growing up in a city, she was taught to be cautious of other people and their motives. The first time an older man asked if she was interested in a "mutually beneficial relationship" was at a train station in L.A. on her way to her aunt's house. Mumbling a quick "no thanks," she ran fast in the other direction. But on the ride to Glendale, she wondered if she'd acted too hastily. She was a woman of the twenty-first century, a pro-sex feminist. This was the year of Cardi B's rise and a number of strip-club anthems took over the radio. Everything, from music to movies to social media, told her that to be sexual was to be free. She worked with women who were in lengthy sugar relationships, saw how the men truly loved her friends, and often asked for very little besides companionship. One woman she knew got a guy to pay for her second degree, sending money for textbooks twice a year. All he wanted in return was someone to have dinner with once or twice a month when he was in town. The idea took hold of her. After all, living in Las Vegas meant men handing out business cards with promises of nude, willing women as you walk down the street. It was lights illuminating billboards of the most beautiful woman imaginable, barely covered with a perfected look saying, *yes, I've been waiting for you.* Sofia would be lying if she said it hadn't hardened her a little, seeing that to be successful was to be sexy and at this point she was neither. Plus, her bank account dwindled more and more each semester. Rice and Top Ramen were all that lined her cabinets, and she was only just starting her second year. Mulling this over during the brief trip in north L.A., she decided she wouldn't be so quick to turn the next offer down once she returned home to Vegas.

A month later, she was approached again. Working as a hostess at one of many Michelin-starred restaurants on the Strip, bumping into wealthy people was common. When a man, youngish and well-dressed, asked her for a kiss on the cheek as she sat their party, she saw her chance.

"Of course," she said with a glint of mischief in her smile. "Fifty bucks."

Without hesitation, he offered her the cash from a full money clip he kept in his breast pocket. As the hours passed, she watched the men order course after course of delicacies: white truffle, oysters, Wagyu beef, and a bottle of scotch that cost half of what she made in a year. The man who paid for a kiss noticed her watching and winked at her throughout the night.

Around midnight she clocked out, the man's number in the pocket of her long black coat. That arrangement was her first. She was naïve and he was relatively young himself—early fifties, handsome in that boyish, American way with hair just beginning to gray. They hadn't laid ground rules and lines were blurred. He began getting overly jealous when she didn't respond to texts right away, and eventually Sofia called it off. But it was worth it: She got a semester of school paid for, a Le Creuset cookware set, and the knowledge of what to look for in the next one. If she was going to be part of the sugar lifestyle, she was going to do it right. She scoured the Internet, found subreddits dedicated to sharing tips on marketing yourself for the match you wanted. And yes, she knew the million ways it could all go wrong. It was impossible to research sugar babies and avoid the articles documenting meet-ups gone sour, body parts of beautiful young women found months later in the woods. These stories, she knew, were the exception. How else could thousands of happy members on the sugar sites be explained? So, she made a profile, careful to hide her face in the public photos.

And she waited.

After some careful observations, patterns began revealing themselves and Sofia knew exactly what these men wanted in their girls. They like the look of long hair, because the women to whom they pay alimony wear the sleek, sharp, chin-length cuts of sophisticated, grown women. Long hair is what girls boast about. They tuck it behind their ears like in the movies. Men like full hips, slender legs, and average heights. No tattoos, at least not visible ones, and no facial piercings. They like soft, curious voices that say I'm smart, but never smarter than you. All they really want, she came to realize, was someone to play along with them, indulge their fantasies of escape. She nodded along expertly, adoration in her eyes as they explained their longing to escape through the desert on a motorcycle with a woman they love. She'd smile encouragingly, like it wasn't the same story every time. Yes, you're very original. A Harley through Red Rock, Moab, Mojave? I've never met a man like you. She did her homework for the role and played it perfectly. Her profile listed her attributes: 5'5",

115 pounds, red hair. Brown eyes. No tattoos, no piercings, no smoking or drug use. Her brand was the devoted student, working tirelessly through school where she was majoring in psychology. She wrote she was looking for a gentleman, sick of the boys around the university she attended. That much was true; she was tired of the boys in her classes with their snickers and snapbacks and endless sense of entitlement. That's what the men she met loved hearing the most. She'd described the many failed attempts at dating college boys and the men from the sugar site would laugh.

"Those were boys, you need a man," they asserted, confident they held depths no one could ever know. Really, though, they weren't much different. The men Sofia met with lied and took shortcuts and blushed the same way twenty-year-olds do. But she wasn't trying to build a life with these men; she was just sick of living off the bare minimum. And they were courteous in ways younger men weren't, chivalrous and old-fashioned with their commitment to her. The majority of the time, after a few months of dating, the men would ask her for a vanilla relationship—exclusivity and all. She politely declined, explaining that she was always clear with her intentions. That's usually when the relationship came to an end and she was back on the site looking for a new arrangement. But this was all before David, the one who messed it all up.

His profile had been as inconspicuous as all the others she stumbled across on that late Tuesday-evening search. They met at a cramped café he frequented in the Arts District, minimalistic in its gray and white designs. Sofia always arrived five minutes late, selfishly loving the look of relief on his face when she finally approached. David was barely taller than Sofia herself and stocky in build. He carried himself like someone who frequently commanded meetings, a confidence she admired. He was much more casual than the ones she met before, ditching the tailored suits for clean jeans and a black T-shirt, a Breitling secured to his tanned wrist. Over the coffeehouse din of steam and gentle acoustic guitars, Sofia and David discussed what kind of setup the other was interested in. They laid out clear rules and expectations, both looking for discretion. She made sure to ask if he was married, a deal breaker for the now twenty-three-year-old, and he assured her that he was recently separated. The conversation was light and natural, and David had a nice smile. They agreed to meeting up once a week, $1,500 PPM, and gifts as he saw fit. With the technicalities out of the way, their relationship began.

Within a month Sofia realized that she genuinely enjoyed being in David's company. Their dates consisted of speeding through Red Rock Canyon in one of his many cars, going to art exhibits, and trips to Seattle or Denver to escape the Vegas heat. They talked consistently, always feeding off of one another. They liked the same music and sports, had similar hobbies, and ate all the same food. Over a few months they began seeing one another multiple times a week, and Sofia would even call out of work to spend the evening with David in his huge, modern house eating pasta and watching old Hollywood movies. He never looked bothered when she shared her input, never acted condescending when they debated politics. David was jealous at times, like others were. He would ask if she had other men supporting her, which she denied, and if she slept with other people, which she once again dismissed. Even though he could tell she was lying, he didn't seem to mind as long as they both stayed safe. Quickly, it became evident that he was different from the others. Sofia refused to share the gory details of her sex life with her friends when they asked about her sugar relationships, often repulsed by the requests some of her men had made. But even that was different with David. In moments of intimacy, he never called her names or yanked on her hair like the others did. He didn't ask her to participate in any elaborate fantasies or request little acts of violence. He just caressed her; David admired Sofia the same way he admired the paintings at a gallery they visited on their second date.

They continued this way for the better part of a year. Sofia was now debt-free and had a sizable chunk of change in her savings. David had even convinced her to apply to graduate programs. She wasn't sure when exactly things began to change, but once she noticed the shift, it was impossible to avoid. If she was going to pinpoint a time, it was when she decided to surprise David with dinner at home when he canceled plans to work late. Pulling up to the gate outside David's house, she buzzed for him from her car. He answered alarmed, asked why she had come all the way out.

"I brought takeout from that Italian place you like downtown," she said. "I figured you'd be too busy to cook tonight."

"Sofia, that's sweet, but surprise visits aren't part of the agreement. I'm in the middle of a meeting."

The line clicked off, the sound of static emanating from the call box. David was concise, so brief at times she felt as though he was suddenly annoyed by her presence. Feeling foolish, she drove home. The takeout sat in her fridge for days before she finally threw it out.

Tension continued to rise between the two. David was busy more and more often, going on out-of-town trips and not inviting Sofia like he usually would. Despite knowing it was wrong, she pushed harder. She became clingy like the ex-wives her past men complained about, but couldn't stop herself from texting him to check in. Even when they were together, David was somewhere else. He found reasons to end their dates early, stopped inviting Sofia to stay the night. Every now and then, though, he'd act like he did in the beginning. He'd twirl a piece of her red locks between his fingers, pull her close to dance in the kitchen, randomly gift her diamond earrings—falsely giving Sofia hope that he wasn't tiring of her.

They'd had one of those increasingly rare good days when the next morning, Sofia woke from a text from David asking her to come by the house that night. She spent the day cleaning, reading, working on a paper—anything to make the time go by faster. Finally, she began to make her way over, a desert sunset blooming above her head. On the way to David's sprawling estate, Sofia found her mind drifting, as it often did, to a teacher she had in tenth grade: Mr. Bishop. They grew close when he taught photography, the one class she enjoyed. Sofia, friendless and painfully shy, sought refuge in his classroom. He taught her how to adjust her camera's settings for photos under the glaring desert sun when capturing plants around Ice Box Canyon Trail, her favorite hike. He showed her the best way to photograph the neon sign welcoming tourists to Las Vegas, different angles to embrace the chaos of Fremont. After a few weeks she started spending all her free time hovering around him like the schoolgirl she was, even began eating lunch with Bishop. They talked about books and music, movies and art. He said that her base state was melancholy, saying it in a way that made it sound like an achievement—yet another way she sailed above her peers. With her big wavy hair and her mom's old band shirts, he told Sofia she looked just like the girls he had crushes on in the early '90s when he was a high schooler. When he called her "precocious," letting the syllables roll off his tongue slowly as he eyed the long braid down the length of her back, she was both ecstatic and unsettled at the attention. The way his gaze traveled the length of her body as he said it, Sofia had the troubling feeling that she could have gotten him to do anything she asked. She would loiter around after class ended, searching deep in her brain for something to talk about. He would print out poems to slip in her textbook when other students weren't looking and gave her his cell number "just in case" she ever ran into trouble.

When these older men began approaching her, years later, of course she romanticized it. How could she not? She was fourteen the first time she watched *American Beauty*, sixteen the first time she read *Lolita*. The teacher who called her precocious lent her his copy of *Lost in Translation* when she was seventeen. When no one was around, he called her his Charlotte. He cast Sofia as his lead. After graduation, he texted her, saying he'd wander like a ghost through all the karaoke bars waiting to find her. She bought the pink wig and everything. Eventually, his wife found the messages and they never spoke again.

This was one of many anecdotes she told the boys she dated in the past. They'd laugh at Sofia when she recounted the tale, playfully mocking and calling her a teacher's pet. How quickly they turn from "Wow, you're kinda screwed up, huh?" with a grin to "Oh my God, you are seriously fucked up" when the effects of her past began rearing its ugly head. But the men she met online never knew any of this. They painted her as the bright, young, pretty thing they wanted. David had been the only one who asked about her life, her past. He never judged her for any of it, just nodded with a look of sadness. Sometimes she'd joke about some of her more emotionally taxing experiences and David would command her to stop. She couldn't count the number of times he pulled away from her, avoiding her eyes as he said, "Baby, sometimes you scare me."

Sofia smoked the entire drive over, ensuring the smell locked in her hair just so David would notice and get mad. When she pulled into the large, concrete circle of a driveway, he was out front waiting for her. Wearing a white button-down and jeans, he looked incredible. His eyes were the blue of models in cologne ads, so intense she had to look away. Pulling her into a one-sided hug, he noticed the scent of Marlboro immediately. When she looked up at him, smirking, thinking she had won, his countenance was that of mild disgust. She could feel him mentally adding this moment to the rapidly growing list of her incompetencies. She didn't realize how big of an ask kindness was until it was withheld, didn't notice how much she craved affection until she stopped receiving it.

"Well," she began, stepping a foot away from David. "Dinner? We can order something and watch one of those westerns you like. You feeling some Clint Eastwood?"

He wouldn't meet her eyes, and she had the sinking feeling she hadn't felt in years: He was about to break her heart.

"I'm just going to say it. I called you over to tell you I'm ending the arrangement." He spoke in the same matter-of-fact voice she heard him use hundreds of times on the phone with people from his company. He held his hands up as he spoke, as though it wasn't really his decision. She knew it was his call, though: David never did anything unless it was what he wanted. Sofia's body language changed, and her eyebrows furrowed in surprise.

"Amy and I are going to try to make it work," he said gently, gauging Sofia's reaction.

"Amy? You mean the woman who's been trying to take half of your shit the past year? The one you do nothing but complain about?" Sofia's voice was high, cracking with the accusations. She was embarrassed by how poorly she was holding it together. He flinched at her language. David always hated how she swore. She paused a moment more before telling him the truth.

"I thought you were going to ask to be exclusive," she said, emitting a self-deprecating laugh.

"I knew you'd be angry, but I was hoping you'd understand." He ignored her last remark completely, a cruelty so casual she felt like a teenager again. He continued.

"Come in and drink some water, relax a little."

He hadn't tried to be patronizing, but Sofia felt small. She actually moved toward him for a second, her body used to falling against his when she was upset. She suddenly remembered a criticism her mom leveled at her once a decade ago about how she always had to pick at her scabs, incapable of ever letting them heal. Small marks were scattered across her body, evidence that she could never just let things be.

"Actually," she said. "I think I'm good. I'm gonna go. Good luck with Amy."

He grabbed her wrist as she turned away, the skirt of her dress flaring out dramatically. She felt ridiculous. Before she could push him back, David was putting an envelope in her hand. Feeling its weight, she knew this was supposed to be a parting gift. Without looking at her, he said: "Take this. Get a new laptop for school. I know you need one."

She considered shoving the cash-stuffed card into his chest, screaming that this meant more to her than money. Instead, Sofia accepted the gift slowly before she stormed to her car and slammed the door shut. She could hear his voice calling for her to come inside and talk, but she knew he wouldn't stop her leaving. She turned her music on full blast and sped out of the driveway, David's back as he walked to the front door the last image she had of him.

As she drove out of the small canyon surrounding David's house, sobs escaped her. She jabbed the volume button off, overwhelmed by the music's intensity. She wondered how she managed to mess up the one relationship she truly cared about. Getting on the freeway, she felt her thoughts spiral before she could stop them, the ones she tried hardest to keep locked away. Did she frame her entire womanhood around men, their desires? The pleasure Sofia received from being seen as both powerful and delicate made her do wild things. It made her crave luxury and excess in a way she never had before. She liked to think being surrounded by extravagance didn't change her, but maybe it had. Sadness, rage, and desperation all ran through her, one after another. Thirty minutes later, she pulled into a parking spot and walked the three flights of stairs up to her apartment. The tears had dried and her face felt stiff. She crawled on top of her sage duvet cover, mascara smearing onto the soft fabric. From her open window she could hear the traffic of overpacked buses and aggressive drivers. Part of the Strip was visible, and Sofia pretended the flashing lights were Morse code telling her to go to sleep.

Sofia woke up at two a.m., exhausted. Her mind was heavy, her body disconnected. The conversation with David left her feeling as though she had jumped into a pool wearing all the designer clothes he bought her, sank to the bottom, then clawed her way out. She checked her cell for the obligatory *Home safe?* text she was used to getting from David after their dates, but there were no new messages. She slipped out of the intricately patterned sundress she'd worn to see him, a last-ditch effort to remind David that, at one point, she was all he wanted. Grabbing her laptop off the dusty side table, she opened up to the site she found David on a year prior. Her account was dormant, but still existed. Letting the mouse hover over "Reactivate Account," she wondered if she could really leave it behind. Lovelorn and miserable, she hit the bold "Delete Account" button, selected "Yes, I'm sure," and rolled back into bed. She fell into a hard, dreamless sleep for a few more hours. At seven, she woke again. Sunlight leaked into the room from behind the curtains, hurting her eyes.

The apartment was empty.

The bed was cold.

In the Wedding Hall

Nicholas Russell

Old days. Your letter says to start with the old days. I'm curious whose you mean. How about this: People were young once, people were old once. At one end, people were born and on the other, gone. Those were the old days, for everyone.

Now, people are young and old and everything in between. Choices, they flower in wondrous, ground-breaking, ordinary ways. These mile markers, a birthday, the day someone quits their job, a day when they do absolutely nothing, these are points in time that have been made flat and tangible like stones on a path. Step forward, step backward, it's up to you. But they're fixed, plucked and carved into glorified destinations.

So you're still young. You're still any age and you

still die. But here, in the wedding hall, you're allowed to gather yourself. Portend, reminisce. The doors open, music plays, and in you walk, all of you, one at a time, from a constellation of moments within your life. Older, softer, weaker, taller, doesn't matter. You've never been a crowd by yourself and now you are. You as a child, as an elderly woman, in college, you unemployed, you pregnant, each one of you an individual apart, grasping hands, pouring drinks, trading glances.

I sweep the floor, smooth the yellow tablecloths, turn on the disco ball, and look at you measure two versions of yourself, a teenager and a middle-aged woman. For these occasions, we only offer one lighting setup: the atmosphere of a garish bachelorette party after everyone's left. A purple hue from bioluminescent paint suffuses the walls so that everyone is backlit into silhouettes. By contrast, the shards of revealing white light thrown from the disco ball poke out bits and pieces of people in startling clarity. An eye, the color of its iris clearly visible. Wrinkles on knuckles. Dandruff on someone's shoulders. It's what I imagine it was like to swim in the ocean, to look up at the sunlight coming through the water.

The teenager smiles as the woman shakes her head in recognition. Details, as she remembers them, just slightly off. A scar not yet cut. Hair tucked behind the other ear. Here you are in the wedding hall, drinking from each other's glasses, telling one another to try this or that, surprised at what tastes you've grown into, delighted by what you remember.

You burst into the wrong bathroom and vomit into a urinal.

It's my second year on the job, I'm twenty-three, and I'm cleaning a handicap stall. I can see your baggy jeans under the privacy shields and a belt too wide for the loops around your waist reflected in the mirror. Seventeen years old, maybe, it's hard to tell with your hair over your face. The mop in my hand slips and clatters onto the tile, but you're still throwing up. Outside the door, a woman calls your name, her voice blurring with the bass of the sound system. Followed by the sharp tap of heels that drift away into the adjacent bathroom until they draw closer and now she's here too. You in your forties, give or take. I've met her before, the tattoo on her shoulder is brand new. She (you) got it (get it) on an authorized excursion back to 2113 before her favorite tattoo artist dies.

But protocols and so on. You can't influence each other's larger decisions in the wedding hall. You can't reveal to a past self what their future self ends up doing with their life. It's restricted, creates all sorts of problems. So you, the younger you, don't know about the tattoo because you haven't been told. The older you has been covering it up all night. But I have to assume, with your head halfway down a sewage pipe, tattoos are the last thing on your mind.

You bend over yourself, stroke your back. She's more than twice your age, but there aren't too many changes. You'll get a little taller, your haircut will change. I can tell she's trying to hide the new ink, bringing her cardigan over the see-through back of her dress. It's a bird, or maybe a reptile, hard to know.

Once, after a long night, when her counterparts had already gone, she helped me clean up the hall. That's not when I fell in love, obviously. But I think of that night often. She wasn't helping out of kindness. Something seemed to have upset her. She absentmindedly piled used napkins on dirty plates and brought them to the janitorial unit. A black-leather jacket hung on the back of a chair and she picked it up, then set it down, twice. I told her I was sorry, but I had to shut the room off and we both reached for the jacket. It didn't feel fated, that brief brush of skin, nor the quiet gasp she and I made at the same time, nor the infinitesimal moment when we looked at one another and knew we could do what we wanted without anyone seeing.

No, it was the way I kept reaching forward, how I handed her the jacket, and the way she looked at me as if she had discovered something. She knew me and tried not to show it, but beyond that, there was something I couldn't place, something more. Fear, amusement, revelation, whatever it was, it was between us. She wandered over to the portal and stepped through without a backward glance.

For a moment, I forget I'm in the bathroom. Then the smell rouses me and I realize my head is sticking up above the privacy shields. You're a teenager and an adult. To one of you, I'm a stranger. To the other, we've been married for almost fifteen years. But I don't know that yet.

You gather yourself, smooth back your hair. You look over your shoulder at me and tell yourself you want to go back outside.

It's easy feeling like time is no longer consequential.

Everyone always jokes that, out of everywhere in the system, Vegas would be the only place where you could safely be a temporal tourist. I used to work at the ballroom underneath the Bellagio, the one place that (legally) allows you to congregate with other tourists from Before and After instead of just other versions of yourself. But that was before they started regulating customer conduct and anyone could do this sort of thing anywhere. People coming and going from all over, revealing anything they wanted, bringing items and people forward and backward, derailing hundreds of millions of timelines. They shrunk it down to Vegas and only Vegas not long after I graduated high school. The Jungle Sanctuary out on the west side, that glorified artificial forest, had finally grown to its minimum acreage by then, despite what the tour companies say. (For some reason, everyone just assumes that patch of brilliant green, in the middle of the Mojave, has always been there.)

I guess I'm telling you all this because I don't know that we've ever talked about the time that made you and me possible. That's all there really is. Sitting beside the days you got with me, there's a bunch you didn't hear about. I don't know where those go. They get lost in the grand narrative of us and, more and more, I'm beginning to tire of always talking about the same few moments from our story. The meet-cute, your proposal, our children. So much of nothing had to happen first. And isn't it strange to you, this unceasing ability to peer into time, and still everything that's occurred feels like it almost never happened? Like it wasn't supposed to happen? Maybe that's just what those without luxury do, overthink and worry.

It's the unwritten law of the town: If you've got money to spend, you've got bigger problems. I didn't have anything to spend then. I didn't know I would. I didn't know about my dad and what would come next.

I didn't know how little time I had left with Tom. I didn't know about our little boy. I didn't know about you, not really. It felt like all I had was work and the desert. I know now how naïve that was.

You celebrate your twenty-fourth birthday at the wedding hall the same week J starts working there. By now, I've figured out which one of you is the primary account holder. She's almost ninety, but you wouldn't be able to tell. Normally, the account holder is the oldest member of the party, but not always. It just coincides that wealth tends to come with age.

I tell J this and he nods, shrugs because it's not groundbreaking information. He's tall like me, dark curly hair that seems unruly, but is actually meticulously groomed. The important thing is he's a fast learner. We get along surprisingly well. I keep thinking about this as I train him, as he cracks jokes the whole time about working in the world's most sophisticated strip mall. I show him the cleaning procedures, how to prep and prime each gateway for arrival and departure, when he can take breaks, how the point system works (accrue enough working hours, earn an hour's worth of time in the hall), how the point system actually works (sick days and PTO subtract points from your record), where to look for extra food on the days he forgets to pack a meal. With each new task or piece of information, he takes to it as if he's already heard about it. Which, in hindsight, doesn't surprise you or me.

Still, he says this is his first job, a service position that, with any luck, he'll matriculate out of in the next four or five years should he decide to stay. It's my third and I still don't know why I'm here. The money is unremarkable, the city is home, but not in a way that compels me to explore it further. What I really do, what actually pays my living expenses, is write, but I don't need to do that here. My family has lived in Vegas for five generations and, though wealth never stacked up the way it did for others, we're recognizable to most of the residents, which earns me a kind of comfort and ease.

These are weak justifications. I could scrounge what I needed to start somewhere else. Still weak. Then, like a raindrop, my calendar updates with the next week's schedule and there's your name and I know I've really been standing at the door with one foot out, waiting to see if I can convince you to come with me.

Here's a day I never told you about.

Greta, the owner, gifts me the business in 2129. I've been here seven years and you and I are living together. Greta says she trusts me not to run the thing into the ground. I often wonder, had I known that this was going to be the payoff, if I would have quit earlier. Seems brash, but I thought the whole thing was too good to be true.

As part of the position, I get the equivalent of a year's worth of time in the wedding hall, exactly 8,760 hours. Or, should I choose to sell the business and cash that time out, around nine million dollars. These hours are, like the money they're worth, finite and only subject to change by the government. And because the risks of temporal business are so plentiful, each hour is extremely expensive. It is both the most generous and most baffling gift I've been given. I refuse immediately. She gives me two weeks to change my mind. That night, I propose to you.

It's been several months since you last visited and left me a letter. You, really you this time, about twenty-nine years old, the one who finally catches my eye and keeps it. In the meantime, other versions of you have passed through, but none of them treats me any differently. Of course, all customer information is private, so I have no way of writing back. But I have to believe we're entangled. I tell J this and he laughs at me. He says my desperation is endearing, sweet. I used to hate being called sweet, but he assures me it's not an insult, says he wishes he could be there to see my face this Friday when you return. He never works when you're here and I hope more than anything it's not because he's embarrassed for me.

In a room full of yous, names get confusing quickly, but you've all naturally gravitated toward monikers that denote your temporal relationship to one another. The older women prefer cute, almost condescending pet names, while those closer in age use single letters or full names. To minimize any revealing details about the future, and to make everyone's lives easier, some of you opt to wear the same outfits every time you visit. In the span of seconds, I can see years of wear. Mended tears. Patterns that fade with use. You're sentimental about a raggedy necklace given to you by a friend, always have been, and each time you come, the chain has been replaced. All these things like hand-me-downs, only literally.

You don't show for over an hour. The rest of you are milling about in pairs and trios while a movie from before you were born plays in the background. It's almost exclusively older women tonight, all of you either retired or nearing it. In the pocket of my vest is my response to your letter, now damp with sweat. At one point, after refilling a table's water pitcher, I trip over a pulled-out chair and drop a glass. It shatters on the floor and, in the silence that follows, I expect awkwardness and embarrassment. Instead, there is a noticeable absence of tension. Instead, it seems as if the room collectively breathes a sigh of relief, as if a moment has finally arrived. Then, one of the gateways behind the projector screen begins to flash its priming sequence and from the darkness, you step through. You're all smiling at each other. You're all whispering in each other's ears.

From the future, I can finally see the absurdity of it all. Every older version of you that came through the hall had to pretend not to recognize me, not to see me as their husband or the father of their child. Rather, as a stranger, younger, naïve, unwitting. Every younger version of you was forced to do the same, ignorant of my eventual significance, though in many ways, a constant fixture in your life. You've been coming to the hall from all periods of your life. I've tended to and served you even before all your baby teeth fell out. I've taken your coat when you were nearly blind with cataracts. And the whole time, I only aged a few years. This night is no more or less significant than the rest. It is simply when the scale tips.

I lift myself off the floor and begin picking pieces of glass up from the carpet. An elderly woman, possibly the account holder, makes her way over to me, lays a hand over mine, and says I don't need to worry about all that. Two others younger than her crouch at her feet and finish cleaning up. You've stepped through the gateway. You've poured yourself a drink and sat next to a woman who, in any normal scenario, would seem to be your aunt.

I'm twenty-five. At some point down the line, as our

baby grows and begins to walk, I'll remember this night and wonder how I could be so inattentive. Jude, our boy, he and I have a serious conversation about the danger of his actions. All this lying about where he spends those afternoons during his senior year of high school, homework or movies or field trips. When, really, Jude was traveling back in time to work with me, a version from before he was born. How, innocent as his intentions were, catastrophe could have struck. He'll try to wring it out of me, the exact date when I drop the glass, but neither you nor I will ever tell him. We save that for ourselves.

Old days. Your letter said to start with the old days. Those were the days.

Sucker for the Witch

By Emily Bordelove

As Mason and Sage locked eyes, tingles spread across her body. She bit her lip to avoid gaping at the most attractive man she'd ever seen while her best friend Soraya closed their apartment door behind him. When Soraya had told her growing up that she had a half-brother she'd never met, she pictured someone like Soraya with warm golden skin, kind brown eyes, and thick hair so dark it appeared almost black. She couldn't have been more wrong.

Mason had fierce blue eyes that were unnervingly pretty, long light-brown wavy hair, muscular arms and shoulders she could see outlined through the tight fabric of his blue polo, and a well-defined ass that his jeans cupped perfectly in all the right places. Soraya had told Sage he was a professional hockey player recently traded from the Detroit Red Wings to the Vegas Golden Knights and had asked Sage to be with her when she met her half-brother for the first time for dinner tonight and Sage hadn't even thought twice about it before agreeing. Now, she wasn't so sure.

Damn, she needed to stop staring.

He'd given her a well-practiced, self-assured smile when he sat down at their small kitchen table. He probably thought he appeared confident, but Sage knew the difference between confidence and cockiness. She knew guys like Mason. She'd dated guys like Mason. She shuddered internally at the memory of Wyatt, a vampire she'd gone out with for six months last year. In hindsight, his only redeeming quality was that he found period sex normal. While there was no denying Mason was hot, she could already tell he was a douche.

No thanks, I learned my lesson.

"What do you do for work?" Mason asked while they were eating dinner.

"I'm a school counselor at Silverado High School," Soraya said after she swallowed a mouthful of taco. "I just finished applying to grad school—well, we both did." Soraya angled her head toward Sage.

"What do you plan to study?"

"I'm getting a Masters in library science and Sor is

getting hers in psychology," Sage said.

Soraya started talking about the different programs she'd applied to, but Mason didn't seem to be listening. His eyes were roving over Sage's body, likely taking in every detail from her straight, deep-brown hair, to the spattering of freckles across her nose, to the way the amethyst sweater Soraya had bought her for the holidays was a bit snug around her chest. Sage glared at him indignantly. His lip quirked up in what appeared to be a challenge. She rolled her eyes and, instead of telling him to fuck off, willed herself to be the supportive friend Soraya had always been for her. She got up to refill her glass of iced tea.

"Do you have any ice?" Mason asked, smiling in an arrogant way that set Sage's teeth on edge.

"Nope, sorry," Sage said. Had Sage's mom still been alive and seen the smile on her face, she would've said Sage's horns were coming out. "I'll fix your drink, though." With a slight flick of her wrist, Sage froze some of the molecules of soda in Mason's cup. "That good or do you want more?"

Mason stood up abruptly, looking from Sage to Soraya and back to Sage again.

"Why do you look so shocked, werewolf?" Sage asked. Her eyes were gleaming at having caught him off guard.

"She knows?" Mason asked his half-sister. His face turned a deep crimson, whether from embarrassment at having broken his calm demeanor or from anger with Soraya, Sage wasn't sure.

"She's my best friend and clearly part of our world," Soraya said, gesturing to his drink.

"How do you know we can trust her?" Mason asked, close to snarling. His mouth was set in a thin line, his eyebrows creased in the middle.

Soraya looked at Mason as if he'd slapped her. "Sage was there when I turned for the first time. Her and her mom told me what was happening to my body, that I'd learn to control it with practice, and that it was completely normal," Soraya's voice broke and though tears swelled in her eyes, she didn't let them fall. "They drove me out to the desert so I wouldn't have to worry about hurting anyone and never left my side. Sage has been there for everything."

He paled, seeming to understand their dynamic, albeit belatedly. "I didn't know."

"Clearly," Sage said, placing her hand on Soraya's shoulder. "If you had only asked, we would've told you," she added.

"How old were you when you turned for the first time?" Mason asked, tentatively.

"Sixteen," Soraya said. "I'd known about the supernatural world long before that, so it wasn't shocking that werewolves existed, exactly. It was more shocking that I was—well, am—one."

Any sorrow that had been on Mason's face after seeing the withering look Soraya gave him vanished. In its place slid his mask of arrogant charisma. "Sage tell you she's a witch?" Mason asked, smirking.

"I didn't actually tell her," Sage said. "I didn't have the best control over the elements then." She shrugged and looked at Soraya. They smiled together at the memory of Jacob getting sprayed in the face by the water fountain after pushing Sage down at recess.

"Care to share a story?" Mason asked, smirking and wiggling his eyebrows in a silent challenge. Sage rolled her eyes and gave in. Placating him with an embarrassing childhood story seemed reasonable.

Both Mason and Soraya pretended nothing had happened after that and the rest of the night passed by uneventfully.

That was a month ago. Since then, she'd attended a couple of slightly less awkward family dinners with Soraya and Mason, as well as a Vegas Golden Knights game that made her blood thrum with energy. Seeing and hearing the sound of Mason check another player into the boards had Sage flushed and sweating in the 50-degree arena, though she was reluctant to admit it, even to herself.

Sage was at work creating delicate wisps of wind to dust the books before placing them back on their shelves when Mason waltzed in, though she didn't notice immediately. She didn't get much of a chance to use her elemental abilities at work, so when it came time to clean and pull liquids out of books that had been spilled on, the world melted away and she savored each stroke of magic singing in her soul. When she glanced up and saw Mason walking toward her with easy, confident steps, he was running a hand through his long hair. After a quick Google search following their initial meeting, she'd learned this hairstyle was known in the hockey world as a "flow" and was basically the same as tattooing "I'm a douche" on one's forehead. She tried to avoid glowering whenever she thought of the word. He was wearing a gray T-shirt so tight she could see the outlines of his muscles and it took all of her self-control not to roll her eyes and reach out to touch his biceps. Soraya had asked her to play nice and Soraya rarely asked for anything.

"What can I do for you, Mason?" she asked in a tone she hoped was pleasant.

"Seen Soraya?" he asked. "We were supposed to meet at my place after work, but she's not answering her phone and her work said she was on her way to meet you."

Sage frowned. "Maybe she wanted to stop by our apartment first. I'm off in ten minutes. I'll go with you. Why don't you get a drink at The Coffee Press?" she said, pointing to the Paseo Verde library's coffee shop. He nodded and walked off.

Ten minutes later when he came back with a large to-go cup of coffee, there were cracks in his façade. He was walking quickly, not his usual languid pace, as if his time was more valuable than everyone else's. He stopped in front of the information desk, his hair askew as if he'd been grabbing fistfuls of it. As his blue eyes met her own, she saw something she never thought she'd see in his confident features—fear.

Sage actively made an effort not to speed down the 215 toward Eastern. Mason, behind her in his own car, was riding her bumper, practically begging her to go faster. Sage only sped when she was late or something was wrong. She wasn't late and there wasn't anything wrong. There wasn't. Soraya was probably sitting on the couch, eating one of the cannolis that they'd bought yesterday from Freed's Bakery to celebrate both of them getting into online programs. Soraya was fine. She had to be.

After pulling off the freeway and turning into her apartment complex, Sage sat repeatedly pressing the clicker clipped to her visor, pretending it was just her natural impatience. The gates creaked opened, agonizingly slow. She quickly parked, got out, and locked her car. Mason was already running up the stairs toward their apartment. Sage stopped halfway up the stairs when she saw Mason standing in front of an already-open door. The lock was still in place, but the upper hinges had come loose. The yellow-green sneaker print of pollen in the center of their door told Sage it had been kicked in. Mason rushed forward, Sage on his heels.

She froze in the doorway and watched Mason rush toward Soraya's bedroom. Sage wanted to race after him, but her feet were glued in place. She could hear her heart pounding in her ears as she tried to take in the details of their apartment. Their IKEA coffee table was cracked in half, their hand-me-down couch was overturned, there were bloody claw marks on one of their walls, and what appeared to be multiple sets of large bloody footprints. Mason rushed back out of the bedroom, his hands balled into tight fists. Sage inclined her head toward Soraya's room, asking him a question neither of them could voice. He shook his head. His eyes widened with terror when he saw the blood and sprinted toward it. Mason gently touched the claw marks on the wall before bringing his hand to his face to sniff his fingers. He sighed and relaxed minutely.

"It's not her blood," Mason said. Sage sighed, happy Soraya had made her attackers bleed.

Any minor relief he felt from the blood not being Soraya's disappeared as he took in the rest of the room. Sage could've sworn she saw what appeared to be anger, despair, and guilt play out on his face.

"Mason," Sage said, quietly. He looked at her, surprised. She wasn't speaking with a delicate kind of quiet, but rather a lethal kind. "What is going on?"

Mason ran his hands through his hair. Sage thought he was trying to hide the fact that they were shaking, but she saw. He looked down at her, their eyes meeting momentarily before his darted away and he began pacing. Patience was not one of the virtues Sage possessed. She rubbed her temples and took a deep breath. Quiet fury hadn't gotten him to talk, so she tried a different tactic this time.

"Mason!" she yelled, grabbing his shoulders and forcing him to look at her. "You know something. Tell me."

"I don't even know where to start," he said, walking over to their kitchen table. He righted one of the upturned chairs before sitting in it and letting his face fall into his hands.

"Start at the beginning," Sage said, firmly but not unkindly. She'd watched Mason and Soraya grow closer these past weeks and she knew he clearly cared for her.

She picked up another chair off the ground before sitting beside him.

Mason was hesitant and slow to speak at first, but once he started talking, it was as if he couldn't stop. He told her that when he was fifteen, his hockey coach had seen him partially transform one night after practice. He'd only transformed for the first time a couple of months before and hadn't even told his dad what he was, so he was learning to control it on his own. Mason didn't know anything was wrong until he showed up for a tournament a few days later when his coach told him he needed to throw the game or he'd tell everyone what Mason was. Mason agreed and spent the game taking unnecessary penalties, fanning on shots as well as passes, and losing puck battles in the corners. He learned later that his coach had bet against their team, the favorite, to win the tournament and had made a lot of money. Since he stopped coaching after that year, Mason hadn't really thought about him again until a few days ago when he received a message from him blackmailing Mason, again.

"I ignored the first one, until I received two more today threatening my sister's safety if I didn't agree, so I agreed immediately," Mason said, emphatically. "But they took her anyway as added insurance." He thrust his phone into Sage's hands and wiped away a stray tear that had fallen down his cheek. Sage read the texts, more horror building in her abdomen with each one. All of the anger that had been bubbling up inside her before Mason started speaking dwindled into nothing. It wasn't his fault, she realized.

"I knew it was wrong when I did it at fifteen," Mason said, deflated and hollow. "I'm an adult now. I didn't want to do it again, so I thought I could just ignore it, since we didn't have a game for a few days." He put his head in his hands. "Feel free to hate me. I hate myself, too."

"Hey," Sage said, gently. She put her hand on his shoulder and squeezed it. "I don't hate you."

He lifted his head up, his shock evident by his raised brows and widened eyes. "You don't?"

"You were just a kid who was blackmailed by an adult you were supposed to be able to trust. He used you and you hated every second of it, so it makes complete sense you wouldn't want to be in this position again. He threatened to destroy everything you spent your whole life working for. I don't blame you." Sage pushed away her own memories about the dangers of an unequal power dynamic.

"We'll get her back," Mason said, with a certainty promising violence to her kidnappers.

"Yes," she agreed.

For the next hour, they sat in the destroyed apartment brainstorming different plans. Sage sent a message to the handful of pack leaders in the city informing them of what had happened and asking to let her know if they heard anything. Soraya wasn't really a part of any of the Vegas packs, though the two of them hung out with various pack members socially from time to time. Sage wasn't sure if the pack leaders would care enough to search for Soraya, especially since a human took her, but she was desperate and needed to do everything in her power to find her friend. Mason asked why she didn't just perform a locator spell, so she had to explain that she couldn't perform spells at all. As an elemental witch, her magic could only create and control fire, water, earth, and air. When Mason asked why she didn't just call one who could perform spells, Sage bit her lip and hesitantly told him about her history with the witches.

She explained that, similar to the various wolf packs in Vegas, there were a handful of covens, too. When Sage was a baby, the one her mom had belonged to excommunicated her. When her mom had tried to join another coven, they all refused. They avoided witch-owned businesses growing up and whenever they came across another witch, they'd pretend Sage and her mom didn't exist. Her mom never told her why she was kicked out and, after she died, the covens continued to shun Sage as if her mother's mistakes were hers as well.

"Jesus," Mason said. "I'm sorry."

Sage waved away his apology and shrugged. The pity in his eyes made her cheeks flush with shame. It was almost enough to make her miss the cocky, obnoxious front she now realized Mason had put up to hide his own vulnerability. If Soraya were here, she would've said it was similar to the "badass-bitch" front Sage wore when someone she loved was hurt.

"You have to try and contact the witches anyway," Mason said, seriously.

She glared at him. "Did you listen to anything I said?"

"This is too important. This is Soraya's life. You have to try."

Sage sighed. She knew Mason was right, but she also knew the witches wouldn't suddenly change their minds about her after twenty-five years. "Fine," she said. "But don't get your hopes up."

When they entered the Occult Oasis, the bell above the door announcing their arrival, Sage was already rethinking Mason's suggestion that it would be harder to turn her down in person. Her hands were sticky with sweat and she hadn't even seen Lorraine or her mother yet. The scent of sandalwood incense dancing in her nose reminded her of her mom's bedroom, making her heart lurch painfully. She belatedly noticed Mason beside her, eyes sparking with curiosity and hands outstretched as if he wanted to touch everything. He'd mentioned he didn't really know much about the supernatural world aside from werewolves, but she hadn't really believed him until now. He clearly had no idea that every Occult Oasis store was run by witches or that they all looked nearly identical. At least, they did online. Sage had never been in one before, but its contents mirrored her mom's house growing up. Instead of seeing her mom's comforting smile, she saw Lorraine's angular face glaring at them from behind the sales counter.

"What are you doing here?" Lorraine asked, before slowly cataloging every single one of Mason's muscles. Her obsidian hair was cut in a harsh asymmetrical bob and her willowy frame was draped in an earth-toned handkerchief dress.

"Soraya has been kidnapped," Sage said, as calmly as she could. She knew if she wanted Lorraine's help, she couldn't get emotional. Lorraine detested feelings and would turn them away without a backward glance if Sage's eyes even welled up. "I know I'm not supposed to be here, but I can't find her without a locator spell."

"It's a shame you're just an elemental witch, isn't it?" Lorraine said.

"That's why I came here, to ask you and your mother

for help," Sage said, willing her voice to remain neutral, pleading even. What Sage didn't mention was that Lorraine had always had a soft spot for Soraya, which is why they were here. Soraya was queer, but she'd steered clear of Lorraine in part because, where the other witches simply ignored Sage, Lorraine antagonized her, and also because Lorraine scared the shit out of Soraya. Lorraine, however, didn't need to know that if it meant getting Soraya back safely.

"You wasted your time," Lorraine said, continuing to scowl in Sage's direction. "I can see why you thought I might help, but my school crush on Soraya is nothing compared to the atrocities your mother caused."

"Please," Mason said, finally speaking. "Soraya is my sister and it's my fault she was kidnapped, not Sage's." When Mason's voice cracked on the words "my fault," she knew they were well and truly fucked. Sage loved the fierceness with which Mason loved Soraya; it reminded her of the way she loved her, too. But Lorraine, evidenced by her scrunched-up nose and sneer, did not. Sage gently pulled Mason from the shop by his elbow, hoping they had better luck at the other two stores.

On the way to the next Occult Oasis location, Sage convinced Mason to go inside alone. She did, however, arm him with the information that this next witch, Andrew, had cheated on Soraya in both a brutal and public way. Hopefully leaving Sage out of it would make it easier for Mason to guilt Andrew into finding Soraya. But when Mason walked back out of the shop ten minutes later, grimacing, she knew he hadn't been successful either. Andrew and he were coming to an agreement on front-row seats to a Knights game in exchange for the locator spell when his coven leader, who Sage forgot was Lorraine's mom, informed him about a 24-hour ban on locator spells for werewolves. Sage chastised herself for forgetting and balled her hands into fists. She wanted nothing more than to punch Lorraine or Andrew, but that would only make things worse.

Instead, Mason drove to the last Occult Oasis in the city. It was managed by one of Soraya's sorority sisters at UNLV, who thankfully didn't belong to the same coven as Lorraine and Andrew. Mason went in alone again, but in the end she, albeit kindly, refused to help him, too. She made sure to emphasize that she loved Soraya and would do almost anything to help her, but she knew if Soraya was missing, that meant Sage was involved and her mother's acts against the covens were just too much.

After exhausting all their options, Sage leaned against the passenger door of Mason's black Ford Raptor and covered her face with her hands. The emotions she'd kept bottled up since Soraya disappeared felt like hands wrapped tightly around her throat. She could feel tears start to pool in her eyes, but she willed the water back into her body. She knew she couldn't do this indefinitely. The dam would eventually break despite her many attempts to repress her emotions in the past. She felt so out of control in every other aspect of her life right now that her tears were something small she could focus on—that and the fury pounding through her veins. The rage and betrayal she felt toward the witches were something Sage had never experienced before. She thought she'd collapse under the weight of it. They'd let Soraya die rather than help her. Soraya was all Sage had left. She couldn't lose her as well.

The thought of Soraya's death had Sage surrendering to her tears, letting them flow freely down her cheeks. She tried taking deep breaths in through her nose and out through her mouth like that grief counselor had taught her to do after her mom died, but they weren't helping. It felt like someone had tied an icy rope around her heart and was trying to yank it out of her chest. She jumped when Mason appeared before her holding her shoulders. She tensed instinctually under his touch. Just because she had been there for him at the apartment didn't mean he was going to respond to her the same way. She braced herself for his cocky façade and a "rub some dirt on it" pep talk, but it never came.

Instead, he wrapped her in a hug she didn't realize

she'd needed. As he held her close, she relaxed into his embrace, feeling almost safe for the first time since her mom had died. When he finally let go, he pulled a small pack of tissues from his pocket and handed it to her. She managed a small smile and thanked him before wiping her eyes, blowing her nose, and stuffing the tissue in the pocket of her jeans. After a long silence of Mason looking at Sage and Sage looking everywhere but Mason, he finally spoke.

"It's not your fault," he said.

Sage laughed humorlessly as tears swam in her eyes again. "The other witches won't help because of who I am, because of who my mom was. There's no one else to blame, Mason."

"How they react isn't your fault, and I know how it feels to have your past come back to haunt you," he said, quietly meeting her gaze. The sincerity and understanding in his bright blue eyes eased some of the tension in her body.

"I don't know what to do," she admitted. Mason took a step forward, their bodies mere inches apart now, and wiped her tears away with his thumbs as he cupped her face in his hands.

"You're Sage Collins," he said. "If there's anything I've learned about you it's that there is no one more fiercely loyal to the ones they love. I have no doubt you'd knock on every door, scour every hotel, and rip the city to shreds if it meant finding Soraya. That's how I know we'll find her."

"I didn't think you'd noticed," Sage said, surprised. All he'd done for the past month was stare at her curves and make snarky comments.

"I hadn't," he admitted. "Until now."

His lips were soft and gentle as they found hers and electricity shot down her spine. She tugged his hips closer, deepening the kiss, and he teased her bottom lip with his tongue before biting it. Sage sighed into him as he moved his hands down her body. The next thing she knew, her legs were wrapped around Mason's waist and her back was leaning against the passenger door once more. She ran her fingers through his hair as he kissed under her jaw and down her throat, agonizingly slow. When their lips met again, heat raced to her lower abdomen and she started to move her hips against his. She was making her peace with the realization that she was going to have sex in a parking lot, again, when she remembered the first time and pulled away.

Mason's brows scrunched in confusion. "Was that—? Did I—? Are you—?" he rambled, his breathing ragged.

Sage smiled. Not so cocky now, it seemed. "You were perfect," she said, giving him the credit he deserved. "I just thought of someone else we could ask to track

Soraya."

The lust faded from his eyes as his attention slowly seemed to switch from sex to Soraya. "You thought of someone else to track Soraya while we were—?" he asked, gesturing to her legs still wrapped around his hips.

She had the urge to laugh, but restrained herself. She didn't want him to feel embarrassed. "I thought we were about to have sex in this parking lot," she said, smiling. "That made me think of the first time I did that when I was in high school, which made me think of the new teacher at Silverado that Soraya befriended, who is also a witch."

"Oh," Mason said, gently helping her down.

"Rain check?" she asked, willing herself to remove her gaze from his swollen lips.

"Rain check," he agreed, kissing her softly before getting into his truck.

When Sage texted Adrianna that Soraya was kidnapped and she needed her help, she responded almost immediately with her address. As Mason drove, Sage bit the inside of her cheek and picked at her cuticles. Adrianna had been in town for a couple of months; surely she'd already joined a coven. That meant that she either didn't know she was supposed to shun Sage, or that she did and planned to turn them down in person, or was ignoring the shunning and would help them.

Sage was really hoping for the latter. She didn't want to deceive Adrianna or get her into any kind of trouble, but if it meant rescuing Soraya, there wasn't much Sage wouldn't do.

When Mason parked his truck in front of Adrianna's apartment, Sage took a deep breath. Mason squeezed her hand and gave her an encouraging smile. They both knew this was their last shot, but he seemed to have faith in her. The thought calmed her nerves enough to open her door and climb out. Sage willed her hands to stop shaking while Mason knocked on the door. Adrianna answered, her long mocha-colored hair flowing around her face in thick waves, and invited them in. After Sage introduced her to Mason, Adrianna offered them something to drink, but when they declined, she ushered them to sit on her couch instead.

Adrianna was hard for Sage to read. She could tell she was worried about Soraya by the furrow between her meticulously groomed brows, but the rest of her face remained neutral. Sage figured she'd better start from the beginning, so she told Adriana about the state Mason and she found the apartment in a couple of hours ago and the texts he'd received from his former coach. Adrianna frowned and looked between the two of them with pity in her eyes. Under normal circumstances, Sage hated to be pitied and probably would've responded by narrowing her eyes or glaring at Adrianna. But now she just hoped Adrianna pitied them enough to help.

"I know about your mom, Sage," Adrianna said, finally when it was clear they had no other details to give her. "I didn't know the first time we met, but I mentioned meeting you to another coven member and they explained."

Sage sighed as unease and relief twisted inside her. She was glad she wouldn't have to deceive Adrianna, but the look on her face indicated that she wouldn't help them either. "Did you want to turn us down in person?" Sage asked, dejectedly.

"No," Adrianna said, quickly. "Of course I'm going to help you. Soraya doesn't deserve to be punished because of what your mom did more than twenty years ago." Sage wanted to leap off of the couch and run into Adrianna's arms, but she resisted the instinct.

"Thank you," Sage said. The icy rope around her heart loosened knowing that they were truly going to be able to get Soraya back. Mason squeezed her hand and smiled at her. Tears filled his eyes, but he quickly blinked them away.

"Sage," Adrianna said, cautiously. "Do you know what your mom did?"

"I don't," Sage admitted. "She never told me. When she died and the majority of witches kept shunning me, I didn't think they'd tell me, even if I'd asked."

"She died?" Adrianna asked. Her eyebrows nearly rose to her hairline.

"Yeah, about six years ago during my and Soraya's sophomore year at UNLV."

Several different emotions passed over Adrianna's face in such quick succession that Sage couldn't decipher any besides sadness and more pity. Great. Sage rolled her eyes internally. She was deciding the nicest way to hurry Adrianna into performing the locator spell when she spoke again.

"Once you rescue Soraya and she's safe, I'd be willing to tell you what I know about your mom," Adrianna said kindly.

"Thanks," Sage said, surprised. "I'll take you up on that. Let's get Soraya back."

Sage handed Adrianna a sandwich bag containing a few hairs from Soraya's hairbrush and tried her hardest not to impatiently tap her foot as Adrianna set up what seemed like an excessive number of candles. As she began chanting in an ancient language Sage didn't know, all the candles lit at once illuminating the map they surrounded. Magenta sparks began circling the Flamingo hotel-casino before spelling out the number 375.

After thanking and hugging Adrianna profusely, she

refused to let them out of her sight without at least a couple of protection spells. It took time Sage didn't want to waste, but she relented, knowing they might need it. Then Sage and Mason climbed back in his Raptor and headed for the Strip.

On their way to the Flamingo, Sage asked Mason what he was going to do about his coach. Mason explained that he'd only ever met one other supernatural in the NHL, a dragon on the New York Islanders, a story Mason promised he'd tell Sage another time. So she clamped down on her curiosity and told him to continue. Mason had reached out to the other player a couple of days ago, after he got the first message from his coach, asking him if he knew of any more of them. He finally got back to Mason today just before he walked into the library and told him that there were around three dozen of them. Not just players but also coaches, general managers, scouts, and higher-ups, too. He put Mason in contact with a lawyer the league employed for matters like this. He left a message with the lawyer and was now waiting for a callback. No wonder he looked so sure of himself walking into the library earlier.

Sage grabbed Mason's hand then and smiled. He was smiling, too, and she could see the relief in the way he held himself. "I'm so glad there are other supernaturals in the NHL, but even if there weren't and you were the only one, you wouldn't be alone. Soraya and I are on your team now."

After stopping at the red light, Mason turned to her, his smile the most genuine one she'd ever seen on him. There was no charm, no cockiness, no sarcasm—just pure joy rippling across his handsome features. When he cupped her face with his hands, the kiss was gentle and sweet, a promise for what was to come once Soraya was safe. His smile after he pulled away rivaled only her own.

When they pulled up to the valet at the Flamingo, Mason handed the attendant a hundred-dollar bill and asked if they could leave his truck parked up here since they were in a rush. The attendant agreed, placing the bill in his pocket, and parked the Raptor between a Maserati and a Porsche. Sage bit her lip to stop herself from gaping at Mason. She wondered if he really made so much money that it was just casual to hand out hundred-dollar bills or if no one had ever taught him how to save or invest.

They walked quickly through the lobby while making themselves as inconspicuous as possible. When the elevator doors closed behind them, Sage realized that they didn't have a plan.

"We need a plan," Sage said, turning to Mason.

"We have a plan," Mason said, calmly. "You're going to use your powers on my coach and I'm going to find Soraya."

"There were at least two different bloody shoeprints in our apartment and both were too big to be Soraya's," Sage sighed. "That means your coach has help. Plus humans love guns. What if they have guns?"

"Do Adrianna's protection spells work against guns?"

"No idea," Sage said, wringing her hands. "I hope so."

When the doors opened, Mason and Sage crept quietly down the hall, keeping an eye on the room numbers as they went. Sage peeked around the corner, her eyes widening. Putting her finger to her lips, she led Mason back a couple of hallways and exhaled deeply.

"There were vampires in the middle of the hallway," Sage said, whispering. She wasn't certain on the distance vampires could hear, but there was thirty feet between them and she hoped it was enough. "Why would your coach hire vampire security?"

Mason shrugged. "How do you know they're vampires?"

"My magic swells when someone near me is supernatural, but vampires are usually easy to pick out since they're so pale and unnaturally still."

"Wait, what's the plan?" Mason asked.

Sage rolled her eyes. Now he wanted a plan. "Vampires hate fire," she said, and figured the rest was self-explanatory. "Don't use your teeth unless you absolutely have to. A werewolf bite is toxic to vampires. It kills them."

"Really, huh," Mason said, eyes wide.

"Don't sound so excited about it," Sage said. "Come on."

Sage was aware the vampires heard their footsteps and hoped they thought they were tourists. They didn't get close enough before for the vampires to smell them, but she was still on edge. The only fangs she wanted near her neck were Mason's. Sage gritted her teeth and appraised the two vampires as they approached them. They were standing in the middle of the hallway wearing suits.

"Welcome, Mason Mitchell and Little Witch," the vampire on the left said. "We've been expecting you." The one who'd spoken was tall, thin, and had red hair. The one beside him was Wyatt, her last boyfriend. Shit.

"Have you been expecting us, Wyatt?" Sage asked, glaring. Mason cocked his head and raised his eyebrow. "Vegas is a fishbowl," she added by way of explanation. "We dated last year."

Sage couldn't decide if the way Mason stood up taller and looked ready to attack Wyatt was sweet or annoying. She restrained from rolling her eyes at both herself for thinking it was even potentially sweet, and Mason for doing it at all. Just because all Mason had seen Sage do with her powers was dust and make some ice didn't mean that Wyatt wasn't aware of what she was capable of when pushed.

"You're going to want to move," Sage said, eyes on the vampires.

"Now why would we do that?" the redheaded vampire asked, smiling.

"Dude," Wyatt said. "You're going to want to move."

The other vampire laughed. "My girlfriend is a witch and put a protection spell on me. Plus what's this bitch going to do anyway? She's barely over five feet tall."

Sage smiled savagely and called fire into her palm. The golden and bronze flames tickled her skin as she felt her magic sing inside her. It had been too long since she'd used this element.

"Last chance," she said. "That includes you, Wyatt."

"Nice to see you again, Sage," Wyatt said, saluting her over his shoulder as he ran in the opposite direction.

Mason openly gaped at her. She would enjoy the look on his face when she and Soraya told him the story together later. She erected a wall of fire between them and the vampire, making sure to keep it from touching either the carpet or the walls, as burning down the hotel was not on today's agenda. She made her way to room

375 and gestured for Mason to open the door. She supposed she could blast it with wind and open it that way, but werewolf strength was much quicker and more efficient. He kicked it down and walked inside, Sage on his heels.

The room was what you'd expect from a three-star hotel, with the basics and the ever-present decades-old stench of cigarettes. Soraya was seated in a chair that had been reupholstered several too many times in the center of the room. Chains were wrapped tightly around her wrists and ankles. She was also gagged with what Sage assumed was one of the room's hand towels. Sitting on the king-sized bed next to her was a greasy-haired man in his early sixties holding a gun pointed directly at Soraya. Sage wasn't sure if Mason's coach knew that the only way to kill a werewolf with a gun was with silver bullets, but she didn't want to take any chances.

"Let my sister go!" Mason yelled, his hands tightening into fists as he looked Soraya over.

"Now, Mason," his coach said. "Why would I do that before you've agreed to my proposition?"

Sage growled at him. She didn't know this man, but she knew his type. She called the fire to her palm again, satisfaction creeping up her spine as the coach paled.

"What are you?" he asked, pointing the gun at Sage

now. "Some kind of witch?"

"Something like that," Sage said. She could see Soraya's blood dripping off of her chains and onto the carpet. She didn't want to kill this man, but if it was him or Soraya, it wasn't even a question. "Put the gun on the ground or I turn you into a pile of ash."

"Not going to happen," he said. "Besides, in order for a witch to attack you, you have to have wronged her and I've never done anything to you."

"Where did you hear that?" Mason asked, looking between Sage and his coach with amusement. Still unsure if the bullets in his gun were silver, Sage didn't correct him.

"You kidnapped my best friend," Sage said, gesturing to Soraya. "And blackmailed my—Mason." Sage could feel the blood rushing to her cheeks and see Soraya's eyes widening with realization. Tension stiffened Sage's muscles. A quick glance at Mason allowed her to breathe a sigh of relief though. He was smirking at her. Of course he was.

"Last chance," Sage said again, directing her attention back to the coach. She increased the height of the flames in her hand for emphasis. This time he did as he was told.

Mason walked over to the gun while his coach backed away, shaking. He unloaded it, showing Sage they were just regular bullets, before putting it in the waistband of his jeans. The coach slumped to the floor, defeat etched in his features. Sage froze the locks on Soraya's chains before she had Mason break them. Once the chains were gone, Soraya started to heal, and Sage felt like she could finally breathe again.

"Why did that guy run away from you?" Mason asked, once he, Sage, and Soraya were sitting in his truck taking the 15 back to their apartment.

"Wyatt?" Soraya asked. "I can't believe he didn't remember me. I wish I could've seen his face when he saw you. Can I tell the story?"

"You might as well," Sage laughed. "I always sound a little too happy when I tell it and Mason might run."

"Hey," he said, meeting her gaze in the rearview mirror. "The only way I'm running is if it's toward you."

Sage's stomach did a little backflip.

The Long-Promised Return of One-Eye Battle

By Brett Riley

Twenty minutes after he had stopped a half-in-the-bag tourist with a newly scratched Toyota from attacking one of the valet guys, Reymundo Arce sat on a bench where people waited for their rides. His head ached, probably from stress. Geez, what a day. He needed to calm himself before going back inside, or he might start Three-Stooges-eye-poking the gamblers.

You okay? asked the valet he had saved, a skinny kid who couldn't have been more than twenty-two. There's something I can get you, just name it.

I'm good, Arce said, though he could have used a beer, or twenty, and a six-year vacation.

Cool, the kid said. I—

Screeching tires coming from Flamingo Road cut

him off. A brand-new Mustang Mach 1 was Tokyo-drifting off the road and into the casino's drive. Pedestrians dove out of the way, some shouting, others flipping off the driver. The car squealed to a halt in the valet lane directly in front of the doors, nearly flattening a guy who had parked in the throughway while helping an older woman out of a rusty 1990 Audi. The man cursed and shook his fist at the Mustang, which was white and dust-covered, windows tinted, engine thrumming like a big cat's purr. Then that sweet growl cut out, and the driver's door opened. A dusty, busted cowboy boot swung out and braced against the ground. The leg attached to it was covered in faded blue jeans with frayed cuffs.

The driver stood to his full height, six feet in those boots. He was thin, face as tan as a baseball glove and lined with deep wrinkles. A gray handlebar mustache framed his mouth and bushed out in all directions. His brown eyes were deep-set and full of an energy the body had gotten no part of; his shoulders slumped, and he moved like a man his age—Arce judged him to be eighty-five, give or take a few years—who had lived hard. He wore a faded, dusty shirt you wouldn't have been surprised to see on a country-music star or a bull rider, all colorful stripes and fake-pearl buttons. He shuffled, as if every step hurt.

Looks like he just stepped out of a crowd scene in

some western.

The guy in the Audi had looked like he might come over and start something, but when he saw the driver's age, he seemed deflated, and he turned back to his passenger, cursing. You just couldn't kick the hell out of some old dude, even if he nearly just killed you.

One of the valets approached the cowboy, who reached into his pants pockets and dug out a crumpled bill. He handed it to the valet, along with his keys.

Rub her down and make sure she's fed, the cowboy said.

The valet squinted at him. Sir?

When you get her to the livery, tell your hostler to brush her till she shines.

Uh, sure.

The cowboy shouldered past and headed for the sliding doors. Arce stood just outside them and nodded at him. Arce nodded at him.

You reckon we'll get any rain directly? the old man asked, nodding back.

Arce hadn't seen a weather report, but when he had come to work, the desert sky had been flawless, the blue so deep it hurt his eyes.

Doubt it, he said.

But the cowboy didn't seem to be listening. He walked into the casino without looking back and turned left, toward the banks of older nickel slots.

What the hell was that? the valet asked.

Wyatt Earp's great-grandfather, said Arce.

He turned and went back inside, his walkie already bursting with staticky calls. Man, what had gotten into people? You could go days without a single incident, and then you got a shift like this, when it felt like all the assholes in the world had agreed to meet in one place and make up for lost time. Well, let the other guys respond. Arce needed five minutes of peace before some half-smashed woman spilled her drink down another one's dress and they started ripping each other's hair out. Life in Las Vegas, where the tourists came in droves because they had been promised a place where they could do things they never would have done at home. None of the commercials reminded people that the town still had laws, that if you didn't act like a decent human being you would face consequences, a fistfight or a security man's hand on your neck or a night in jail. Hell, even that old cowboy probably needed a talking-to. Arce had no idea whether he had been drunk or stoned or just caught up in some memory from when he had been younger and strong, from when he had ridden a real horse under an open sky, but you shouldn't come within a few feet of stampeding people with a car you had no business driving and just walk away.

Yes, it had already been a hell of a night. Earlier, he had stood near the keno tables here in the Sagebrush Gambling Hall and watched a guy in a Hawaiian shirt dig his grave. This dude had been borderline stalking a woman in a gold lamé dress all night. Not that the fabric was legit—if she had been rich enough for the real thing, she would have taken her money and her big hair and her six-inch Jimmy Choos to the Strip, probably the Wynn or the high-stakes tables at the Aria. Instead, she had come to this dingy, Western-themed off-Strip joint where cigarette smoke floated to the ceiling and stayed there because the ventilation system had last been updated in the early '90s. The carpet needed to be shampooed a hundred times, or maybe just burned. The miserable-looking women who carried trays of drinks wore short-skirt versions of what you might have seen on a saloon whore in the same kind of low-budget movie old Mister Cowboy belonged in. Half of the slots here were new and shiny, the other half as outdated as everything else. And the clientele: people in awful shorts and faded T-shirts; elderly folks hauling around oxygen tanks in one hand and tobacco products in the other; guys with way-out-of-their-league women, almost certainly escorts, on both arms and a ton of product in their hair; families with harried parents and snotty kids who always seemed to be running. A $19.99 dinner buffet that might have been worth half that, a wheezing Subway and a staggering McDonald's and a Sbarro with what looked like the world's oldest leg of God-knows-what turning on a vertical spit. A dim movie theater with six screens, all showing second-run features.

Cowboys, for Christ's sake. Arce supposed he should have counted his blessings; at least it wasn't Ninja Turtles or some borderline-racist Chinese pagoda shit.

And sure enough, Ms. Fake Gold Lamé had eventually stood up and wagged a finger at the drunk guy, who recoiled, his eyes wide, his expression saying *Jesus, lady, what the hell did I do?* He had retreated as she marched him down, her voice carrying, though Arce hadn't been able to make out the words. When the guy finally bumped up against the wall, he looked like he wanted to flatten himself out and drop a bucket of paint on his head to blend in. Arce had stepped over and escorted the woman away before she or the guy got physical, telling her that the man wouldn't bother her anymore, and here were some drink coupons she could use at the bar. When he had gotten her settled at a different machine, Arce had gone back and found the drunk guy and advised him to leave her alone. Maybe even take his business elsewhere or, if he was staying in the hotel, sober up in his room. The guy staggered away, still dazed. Just another late-afternoon encounter in the

Sagebrush.

Now, as Arce slow-pursued Mister Cowboy, one of the servers walked by, a fortyish blond named Cherry, or something like that. She and Arce locked eyes for a moment. She dropped him a weary wink and half-smiled. The expression and the gesture combined to say something like, *This shift will never end.* It sure felt that way. Already Arce had broken up a chest-bumping slap-fight between two dude-bros, had escorted three middle-aged women back to their rooms as they stopped to puke in every third trash can, had bum-rushed a rank and dirty homeless guy with wild hair and crazy eyes after he interrupted two poker games and three slot players, asking for a handout. Sometimes it was hard to know how to feel about the people he dealt with. Half of him wanted to put them in an Uber headed for the airport before they got any worse, lost more money, suffered alcohol poisoning. The other half of him could have tossed them into traffic just to get them out of his face.

Or maybe he was just tired. What a day.

Across the way, in a bank of slots that must have been new around the time Jimmy Carter was president, a blue-haired woman who looked about eighty had taken a seat on a showgirl-themed machine, the display bright and cartoonish, the characters so busty they defied gravity. As for the old woman, she hunched over like her spine had started to curve. That bluish hair poofed around her skull like cotton candy. She couldn't have weighed more than a hundred pounds and wore a flower-print blouse and checked slacks, like something you'd see on 1970s retro night at the club. She inserted her slip and started plunking the buttons, a half-smoked cigarette in her free hand, a fresh beer with an inch of head between her legs. She would probably die of emphysema or cirrhosis before she won anything more than a few dollars, but hey, whatever floated your boat.

Mister Cowboy stopped and stared. Oh Lord, was he looking for a date?

Arce's walkie buzzed, and the voice of Leolani Noelani squawked out of it. Rey, said Leo. You free?

Leo was a Hawaiian about as wide as a refrigerator, MMA-trained and no-nonsense. Plus, as head of security, he was hard to ignore. Not even when you felt tired enough to curl up on a roulette wheel and let it spin you like a merry-go-round.

Yeah, boss, Arce said. What you need?

Valets said you're on some geriatric cowboy who can't drive for shit. That right?

Got eyes on him now.

Keep him out of trouble.

Copy.

Arce clipped the walkie to his belt and kept maybe fifteen feet between himself and Mister Cowboy. Probably a harmless old man, when he wasn't driving too much car for him to handle, but still.

The old man started forward again, and yes, he seemed to be heading for Ms. Emphysema Cirrhosis. She had gotten a fresh beer and stubbed her butt. She looked like a chain-smoker, all those spiderweb lines around her mouth and the yellow teeth and fingernails. With her right index finger, which ended in a long nail painted bright red, she was pushing buttons over and over, not even looking at the results.

Mr. Cowboy stopped behind her and took off his hat, a ten-gallon job almost as old as he was, and held it against his chest with one hand. Arce stood to the right of the aisle and watched him, trying to anticipate what he would do. After a while, the cowboy put on the hat again. His tense body language suggested he was gearing up for something, but what? Arce slipped up the aisle and stood right behind him, in case he or Ms. Emphysema Cirrhosis did something crazy. The way this day was going, the old guy would probably strip naked and twerk.

Tillie? said Mr. Cowboy. His voice was high-pitched, hesitant.

Ms. Emphysema started and nearly dropped her

beer. Clutching it with both hands, she turned, scowling. When she spotted Mr. Cowboy, her eyes widened. She opened her mouth, then closed it again. Her brows knitted. She squinted, frowning now. Yeah? she said in the deep, hoarse, gravelly voice of the lifelong smoker.

I knew it was you, said Mr. Cowboy. He sounded choked, like the words were too big for his mouth.

Who are you? Tillie asked.

Why, it's me, he said, stepping closer. Walker.

Tillie studied him for a while. You ain't Walker, she said. You're just some old man.

She turned back to her machine and punched the button again. The man named Walker took off his hat again, crushed it in his hands, kneaded it. *Old man*, she had said. Jesus, what did she think *she* was, some kid at her *quinceañera*?

The fellow calling himself Walker shuffled even closer, hat still wadded in his hands and held in front of his waist. Arce paced him. Surely something was happening here; the woman seemed to know a Walker, even if she didn't believe she knew *this* Walker.

Yo, Pops, Arce said. Mister Walker.

The cowboy turned. His eyes glistened. One tear fell down his cheek. Yeah?

He ain't my Walker, said Tillie without looking at them. My Walker had dark hair, almost black, and a full beard.

Not no scraggly mustache. Strong arms. Thick thighs.

You okay? Arce asked the cowboy, ignoring Tillie. Anything you need? Maybe you wanna walk with me to one of the bars. Get you an adult beverage.

I come all the way from Montana, Walker said. Me and Tillie made a promise forty years ago to meet here, if we was still alive and this place still standin. So here I am. Can't just walk away.

Another tear fell. Whatever Arce had been expecting, this wasn't it. What to do?

Me and my Walker, we was both married, said Tillie. Arce had to move closer to hear her over the slots. My husband was Walker's wife's brother. Dreadful man. Beat the hell outta me until he dropped dead with his fist still knotted in a leather belt with a rodeo buckle the size of an apple. But Walker, he never come for me. Guess he chose his Mae after all, even though she was a damn shrew. I miss his singin. He knew all of Marty Robbins. Townes Van Zandt, too, and Hank Williams, and Merle Haggard.

Arce looked at the old man and raised an eyebrow. That sound familiar, Pops?

Her husband Elder was an ass, Walker said. But his sister, my wife Mae, she warn't so bad. Tongue like a bullwhip, but she stood by me till she died, even after I told her about Tillie. Wouldn't let me outta her sight, but she honored her vows. Wouldn't talk to Elder for the rest of his sorry life, neither, what with his drinkin and his temper. She still loved Tillie, even if she cut her outta our lives.

Oh, yeah? Arce said, unsure of how else to respond. The old dude seemed heartbroken, the woman confused, and nobody had trained him to fix shit like this.

That awful Mae, Tillie said, still plunking the buttons. A server passed, and Tillie ordered another beer. Then she turned and wagged a finger at Arce. A rabid dog wouldn't have bit that bitch. Walker should have left her. I should have left Elder. But our generation frowned on divorce, and we was stupid enough to go along. Only got one life, and we wasted it on shitheads.

She turned back to her game. Walker transferred his wadded hat into one hand and reached out with the other, tentative and trembling, until his fingers brushed Tillie's back. Then he yanked away as if she had scalded him. Forty years ago—this place would have been new then. Arce, who was thirty-two, could barely imagine falling in love with your in-law and longing for that person across four decades, spending every day with someone else you either couldn't stand or only tolerated, seeing another face when you boned, trying to fill that hole in your middle with whatever life brought you, never really succeeding, until one day in your old age you remembered a promise and drove across all the states that had separated you from your true love just like time and circumstances had, only to find that the person you sought refused to believe you were actually you. What would that feel like? What would it do to a person?

Look, Arce said, turning to Tillie. This guy could be your man. Have you seen him since your sister-in-law stopped talking to your husband?

Tillie pushed the button and won over seven dollars. She pushed it again and lost two. The server brought the fresh beer. Tillie drank some and fixed the glass between her thighs.

No, she said. It wouldn't have been proper. Say, did you know my Walker had a nickname?

Arce turned to the cowboy. You got a nickname, Pops?

The old man stood straighter, a little taller. He looked dignified. You're damn tootin. My name's Walker Battle, but they call me One-Eye.

Arce looked into both of Walker Battle's brown peepers. But you got—

Yeah? said Battle, his chin raised in defiance.

Never mind, Arce said. He felt sure there was a story there, but asking about it would only drag all this out even more. Ma'am—Tillie, right?

She glanced at him. You got cotton in your ears? Tillie Bird.

Okay. Tillie, he says his name's Walker *One-Eye* Battle. You know that name?

Of course I do, she said, as if the question were the dumbest she had ever heard. That was my Walker's name, all right. But he wasn't some old man.

Jeez, does she really think her old boyfriend would have stopped aging? Or is she still young in her mind? Dammit, this kind of shit ain't in my job description. And yet something wouldn't let Arce walk away. He wanted to know how this little drama would end.

So, he said to Tillie. How can this guy prove he's who he says he is?

I got my license, Battle said. He pulled out an ancient leather wallet stuffed thick enough to choke a horse. He opened it and worked an ID out of a plastic shield. Arce looked at it. Walker Battle, six-foot-one, one-sixty-eight, brown eyes, restrictions include glasses and no night driving. God must have been riding shotgun in that Mustang, because it was getting dark outside, and Battle had no glasses.

Arce took the license and held it in front of Tillie's face. Look, he said.

She squinted at the license, frowning. After a moment, she waved it away. That ain't Walker, she said.

Arce turned to the old man and shrugged. I don't know what else to do, Pops.

The old man looked at the back of Tillie's head for a while, his mouth working, his eyes still wet, though no more tears fell. Who knew what he was thinking? If his story was true, he had been riding through his own personal West for longer than Arce had been alive. At his age, he had probably outlived health scares, most of the people he had known, much of his family. Now, after all those years, he had ridden straight to his true love on the only kind of horse he could get—and Arce believed that he was Tillie's Walker, because what were the odds that one man of that name had promised to come here forty years ago and another had shown up?—and now the woman he had dreamed of all that time didn't recognize him.

Hell, it made Arce want to cry, too.

Then Battle opened his mouth and sang.

Despite that high, soft speaking voice, he crooned in a rich baritone that carried above the slots and the conversation with the kind of volume that struck you like something physical, made you jerk and widen your eyes. It was the voice of a much younger, stouter man, and it wavered at the ends of the verses and grew even stronger on the chorus, twanging and drawling just like those guys on the casino's playlists. Arce didn't recognize the song—he liked country music about as well as a metal spike through the ear, tried to ignore what he heard at work every day—but Tillie did. Something about a guy named Pancho and his buddy, Lefty. Outlaws, it sounded like, who, despite hard times, stood by each other to the very end.

After the first few words, Tillie stopped pushing the button. After the first verse, she turned. After the first chorus, her beer fell to the carpet and splattered and pooled there, the worn fabric not even absorbing it. After the second verse, she stood. And Arce would have sworn she looked younger—some of those wrinkles shallower or erased entirely, her eyes clearer, her smile suggesting she had just remembered happiness and how it made you more beautiful than you could ever have been otherwise.

She wrapped her arms around Battle, who smiled down at her as he finished the song, and they swayed together as if they could hear the music. Maybe they could.

There you are, she said, her voice almost too low to hear. There's my Walker. You sound exactly the same.

I told you I'd come, he said, and for just a moment, Arce saw the younger One-Eye Battle, confident and tough before sadness and the years overcame him. Even if Mae was still alive, I'd have come. We waited so long, didn't we?

Now Arce really did feel his eyes moisten, his chest

hitch. *Nope,* he thought. *Not gonna cry. I'll never live it down if I do.* But wasn't that the other side of Las Vegas? Yeah, some people came for the fantasies. But surely others chose this city to figure out who they had already been all their lives. To meet their true selves, finally, and shake hands. Maybe even grab hold of love after a lifetime of keeping it at arm's length.

Battle and Tillie leaned in and kissed. Not just a meeting of the lips, but a full-on French kiss, as if they were still young and had all the time in the world.

Aww, someone said.

People clapped and snapped pictures with their phones.

The old folks kept kissing. One of Battle's hands stole down and gripped Tillie's ass. She grabbed the hair on the back of his head with both hands.

Um, someone said.

Battle used his other hand to cup one of Tillie's breasts. She let go of his hair and squeezed his crotch. Their kissing grew more urgent, desperate. Tongues flew everywhere.

Get some, grampa, somebody said, laughing.

Okay, okay, Arce said, taking them each by a shoulder and pulling them apart. Save some for later, you two.

Battle winked at him. Tillie cackled and slapped her

man on the ass.

What say you show us where a couple of old cod-gers can get em a room? Battle said.

I already got one, Tillie said. She reached into the pocket of her slacks and brought out a keycard. It ain't the honeymoon suite, but it's got a sturdy bed. You wanna test it out?

I'd be obliged, Battle said. He winked at Arce again and let Tillie lead him away, toward the elevators.

Arce shook his head. He hoped the two of them would survive the night.

Now his walkie squalled, and Leo's voice bawled out. Rey. Got some chick dancing on a baccarat table in zone two.

Arce got the walkie and pushed the talk button. On it, boss.

He looked back toward the elevators one last time. Battle and Tillie were gone. Arce grinned and headed for zone two. If he was lucky, he would get there before the dancing woman fell off and broke her neck.

Love Dunes

By Krystal Ramirez

Editor's Note: Instead of using language to shape a linear narrative in the reader's mind, Krystal Ramirez reimagines words as art, repurposing them as visual symbols meant to invoke an emotional response. With "Love Dunes," a series of six works, the artist conveys the fractured sensation that love instills in us when we stutter, ramble, or go silent in the presence of our beloved. Indeed, the shapes and movements of these poems speak to the ways that romance can sometimes enervate and overinflate us.

What influenced Ramirez to create these images?

She explains, "I bought a typewriter a few weeks ago and started doing something similar to Carl Andre's concrete poetry."*

Given this book's theme, Ramirez adopts a method that is bewitching and bewildering. Words are crammed tightly together and typed over other words, resulting in moments of palimpsest that speak to the aggressive, obliterative, messy impact of affection and heartbreak. Words are sculpted into thin vertical lines, then later expanded into textured blocks of blurred language. And in one particular work, a six-letter word explodes into a constellation—fragments of the heart in the aftermath of intimacy.

Ramirez's works hold our gaze; they compel us to apperceive love's tenderness and treachery, its destructive and regenerative aspects.

* Andre is an American minimalist artist best known for his sculptures and for his concrete poetry, a visual approach to verse that emphasizes typographical effect over meaning.

ESSAYONSCULPTUREINTHEDUNESBYKRYSTAL

all	bet
hard	time
world	limit
desire	brutal
leave	dream
slow	wing
bow	eve
come	neon
guilt	serve
battle	fuming
bourn	queen
line	mold
cry	all
soft	fine
build	touch
groove	tinsel
night	trust
gold	tear
old	sew
lace	sand
realm	black
suffer	valley
smoke	light
star	gore
you	see
dirt	word
river	cruel
excess	canyon
calor	solas
rust	fool
row	cut
hard	coke
water	vet
source	tail
bound	ditch
king	stucco
run	swirl
mori	coil
blood	set
sparks	feel
white	pleat
plot	gather
cloud	crimp
kisses	tuck
shine	row
sick	show
sky	ill
pink	work
flush	glare
violet	luster

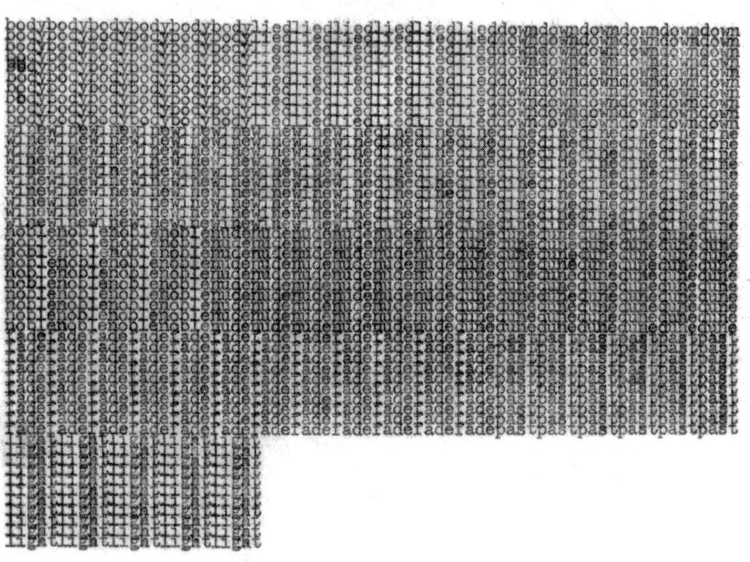

yyyyyyyyyyyyyyyyyyyyyyyooooooooooooooooooooooooouuuuuuuuuuuuuuuuuuuuuuuuu
uuuuuuuuuuuuuuuuuuuuuuusssssssssssseeeeeeeeeeeeedddddddddddddddddddddddddd
tttttttttttttttttttttttttttttttttttttoooooooooooooooooooooooooooooooooooo
bbbbbbbbbbbbbbbbbbbbbbbbeeeeeeeeeeeeeeeeeeeeeeeeeeeeeeeeeeeeeeeeeeeeeeeeee
sssssssssssssssssssssssssssssssssssssssssssssssssooooooooooooooooooooooooo
pppppppppprrrrrrrrrreeeeeeeeettttttttttttttttttttyyyyyyyyyyyyyyyyyyyyyyyyy
iiiiiiiiiiiiiiiiiiiiiiiiiiiiiiiiiiiiiiiiiiiiiiiiiiiiiiiiiiiiiiiiiiiiiiiiii
nnnnnnnnnnnnnneeeeeeeeeeeeeevvvvvvvvvvvvvvveeeeeeeeeeeeeeeerrrrrrrrrrrrrrr
llllllllllllllllllllllllliiiiiiiiiiiiiiiiiiiiiiiiiieeeeeeeeeeeeeeeeeeeeeee
wwwwwwwwwwwwwwwwwwwwwhhhhhhhhhhheeeeeeeeeeeeeeeeeeeennnnnnnnnnnnnnnnnnnnnnn
iiiiiiiiiiiiiiiiiiiiii
lllllllllllllyyyyyyyyyyyyyyiiiiiiiiiiiiiinnnnnnnnnnnnnggggggggggggggggggggg
                         dddddddddddddddddddddddddddddddddddddd
                         oooooooooooooooooooooooooooooooooooooo
                         wwwwwwwwwwwwwwwwwwwwwwwwwwwwwwwwwwwwwww
                         nnnnnnnnnnnnnnnnnnnnnnnnnnnnnnnnnnnnnn

u

b

r

e

a

d

Krystal Ramirez

                L
                OV
                E
                WO
                RD
                SN
                E
                    O
                    N
                AN
                D
                DI
                RT
                HO
                W
                    D
                ID
                WE
                G
                    E
                T
                    H
                ER
                E
                    I
                RE
                LI
                EV
                ED
                    Y
                OU
                AC
                TU
                AL
                LY
                        I
                S
                    T
                IL
                L
                    D
                O
                    I
                CH
                OO
                SE
                    S
                A
                DN
                ES
                S

                                                          CHERRIES
                                      PENNIES

          MOTHER
                                                            FATHER

                                                            DARK

                                                            DARK

                                                            LIGHT

              SEARING
                 BLISTERING
                      SIZZLING

                           HOT
                           HOT

                                        BLUEBLUEBLUE
                                        BLUECOTTONCA
                                        CANDYPASTELS
                                        BROWNTANRUST
                                        REDCRIMSONOR
                                        TANGERINESAC
                                        CHARINESKIES

              DOLLAR   TREES

                             PAST
                             PAST

                  ME
                       ME
              ARGON
                             ASPHALT
                                  DIRT
                       ME
                             AND SUNSET ROAD

A Song for Many Voices

By Heather Lang-Cassera

Above the dunes northeast of the city, the whales
swept through the sky. They waved their tails in contin-
uous movements, just like they once had in the ocean.
They were not concerned about outdoing the fuel-pow-
ered, air-cooled, human-driven shadows beneath them.
Yet, once a creature engaged, they always matched
the sandrail's speed. This was, perhaps, the only way in
which they were similar. Otherwise, whatever the driver
below them did, they did just the opposite. If wheels
carved left, they arced right. If the vehicle ascended a
hill in a large switchback pattern, its whale would oscil-
late groundward like a falling leaf, resembling a rudder
stall. If the dune buggy caught air, the belly of the whale
would, just barely, graze the sand nearby for less than a
moment, somehow leaving no trace, although the grift-
ers, the rogue enthusiasts, and the scientists all agreed

on this observation. For as skeletal as each sandrail was, the fleshy bodies of these overland mammals more than made up for the emptiness of the desert.

For many reasons, it was no surprise that Brendan volunteered for this new unprecedented field assignment. It was solitary work, mostly, and she loved gathering bio-acoustical data—oceans, dunes, sonograms. Brendan found waves beautiful, almost breathtaking.

Brendan's first job after college, more than a decade prior, had been as a North Pacific Ocean observer on a commercial fishing boat. She had been excellent at species identification and data collection and was even better at swimming in a survival suit and righting a capsized life raft. The area in which she was less success-ful was diplomacy, but her interpersonal skills improved, somewhat, within dangerous environments.

Brendan's mother was also a conservation biologist. She met Brendan's father while working in the Mojave Desert conducting desert tortoise surveys and monitor-ing construction sites for the preservation of the threat-ened species. It was a program to pay back her tuition. Meanwhile, while there, Brendan was both conceived and born. She could not remember her father, and her mother did not talk about him. Brendan did, however, have a notable earliest memory, that of a man hum-ming a distinct tune while holding her. She had decided that, in a way, maybe this moment could be enough. When Brendan was seventeen, her mother passed away unceremoniously in an accident on the highway.

But all that was long before. That night, Brendan lay, amidst the dunes, beneath the desert sky. She was over-due to fall asleep by more than a couple hours. Brendan struggled. She blamed her shortcomings in sleep on the erratic schedule she was required to maintain as an oceanic observer. However, she slept poorly before that, too. When she was a child in Southern Nevada, skyglow had already been proven, irrefutably, to disrupt circadian rhythms.

That night, as usual, Brendan tried counting whales. Then she attempted a deep-breathing exercise. For the first many years of her life, she believed that taking a deep breath required pulling in your abdomen. Breathe in. Belly in. She did not think twice about it, not until the pediatrician noticed her daughter, Maddie, barely more than two-and-a-half years old, doing exactly this. "Breathe in, belly out, sweetheart," the physician cor-rected her child. Who would want to push their warm, delicate skin into a cold stethoscope? Brendan thought. Of course she would shiver away from the strange, clin-ical device. Later, though, when her daughter blew out her three candles on her birthday cake, when she made a wish on a dandelion head, and when she woke up panting after a night terror, Brendan knew. She wondered what other failings she might have already passed along to her daughter.

While in the dunes, Brendan kept a photo tucked into her breast pocket, a fading Polaroid. In the photo, no one acknowledged the camera. Her husband looked down, lovingly, at Maddie who was held up by the palm of her father's hand. She was only seven months old, and he would leave them not long after. In this moment, however, his hand, a pulpit of flesh, allowed gravity to press the infant's soft belly toward the sky as her body touched, barely, the surface of the pool water. Better this than drowning, Brendan thought. Better this than not being held. The photo smelled both clean, like chlorine, and murky, something like machine oil.

After her husband left, Brendan had given up the field work she loved, having become a single parent who needed to be close to home. Brendan looked at the photo, holding it near a small camping light, and she allowed herself to touch her husband's mustache, something she did not often do. She worried the residue on her hands would fade the picture. While the two were still a couple, Brendan would joke that, while some babies' first binkies were a blanket or a pacifier, their daughter's would be the very mustache on her father's face. If something looked real, it was real, Brendan told herself. That was all that she could let matter.

Brendan looked toward the sky. She closed one eye and traced the body of a whale with a fingertip. Then she traced another, and another. She thought about how, years ago, she and Maddie would lie on their backs in the grass tracing the outer edges of the clouds any chance that they could get. Cloudy days were rare.

"This cloud," five-year-old Maddie pointed. "It looks like a turtle." She beamed. "Or wait … is it a tortoise? It's not in the water, so it's a tortoise, right?"

Brendan kept to herself that tortoises are turtles. Moreover, she kept it to herself that, yes, this cloud, a cumulus stretching, not too lumpy, more aerodynamic, looked more like a sea turtle than a desert tortoise.

"Well, sweet girl, neither can fly. Do you know what that means?" Brendan suppressed a smile.

Maddie shook her head, her eyes wide and her hair messy.

"It means that …" Brendan tried to look serious before cracking a giant grin. "It means that it can be either." Brendan brushed her daughter's bangs out of her eyes, making note that she should trim them. "Which would you like it to be?"

"A tortoise," Maddie giggle-shouted. "One like Grandma studied."

"Perfect," Brendan replied. "Yes, just like Grandma

studied." Maddie had never met her grandmother, but in some ways, Brendan thought that was okay. She loved sharing the parts of her mother that Maddie could admire, omitting the harshness, her overemphasis on facts over feelings.

In the dunes, there was no grass. Instead, Brendan winced as she shifted her weight within her sleeping bag against the craggy ground. She had started to overnight away from her truck, her trailer, and her sandrail, hoping that they might be the most immediate targets of attention, should anyone be nearby. During the day, the desert glistened with trash, broken bottles, plastic bags. That is the thing about the desert; it can make just about anything shimmer. And at night, her body, within its dark taffeta cocoon, blended in perfectly. If anything, she might be mistaken for a body bag, and when people think that you are already dead, you have the advantage.

Anyway, another broken truck window, she could live with that. Another fractured bone, she would like to avoid. It was hard to climb around installing and fixing acoustic-monitoring anchors with a broken rib. Even if a looter had a center punch or a ceramic spark plug to throw at the window for a smash-and-grab, she had rigged an electrode to sense the sound of cascading glass to wake her up immediately. The equipment that was not deployed was stored in the truck's in-floor compartments. Above them, she had laid carpet from an abandoned vehicle. Otherwise, Brendan had little of value. Fortunately, it was not her job to process the data. She only collected it. Brendan wondered if the analysts knew how much artifact they would be working around; from gunshots to OHVs, illegal activities weaved themselves into the theoretically protected soundscape.

Lying on her back, Brendan watched the whales as they slept. She admired whales for countless reasons, one being their ability to sleep with one eye open, to keep half of their brain awake, an excellent preservation tactic and a way to make sure they never lost sight of their pods. Brendan liked to think of the whales as sleepwalkers, even if the science beneath the metaphor was not quite right. Moreover, the creatures looked a bit like pieces of timber floating together, in formation, along invisible night-sky waterways. Brendan had seen a photo of timber rafting in a library book a few months before. She regretted using those pages as kindling and wondered if the whales' eyes looked like knots of wood, or if time had faded that memory, too.

Sleepwalking was something that she herself had done, apparently only once, splashing milk across both the kitchen table and floor. Her husband had, endearingly, called her the Milky Way. It was a saccharine pet name that did not last.

That night, in the desert, beneath the stars, as Brendan's mind traversed so much history, she thought also about the scientific term, somnambulation, a word she had heard on the radio back in the first year after the catastrophic tragedy, when station programming was set to loop. She thought about how long it had taken her to find the entry in the encyclopedia at that abandoned library. She was sure the word started with sun, and it was beautiful to her to imagine the day-star drifting, still, throughout the night. Brendan felt foolish when she realized that the word was spelled as it was, especially as a scientist expected to know some Latin. Yes, *ambulare* meant to walk. *Somnus*, however, was to sleep. Of course, Brendan thought, flashing back to a memory in which her mother questioned, "Are you sure you want to be a scientist?"

Brendan wondered if the whales would reproduce in their new, strange environment. She wondered if her organization would add this inquiry to their research. Years ago, Brendan had been trained to use a crossbow to collect tissue samples in the North Pacific. A specialized dart would break the skin of the whale, remove a few centimeters of blubber, and then eject itself into the water. The dart, which then contained a biopsy sample, would float so that it could be collected by scientists.

Those samples, Brendan's darts, were used to analyze pollutants. However, this technique had also been used to measure whales' hormone levels, determining reproductive cycles and even pregnancies. Most whales' bodies were too round, already far too abundant, to simply observe a pregnancy. Brendan hated shooting the whales, even with darts. Although she yearned to know if these Mojave whales would be reproducing, she was also glad that she had not been asked to collect anything other than bioacoustical data, and to do so noninvasively.

When her own daughter had turned five, Brendan enrolled her in voice lessons. At first, the instructor told Brendan that five was too young to begin formal training. However, Maddie sang day and night, despite her poor breathing, and Brendan, being someone who knew too much about bad habits, made an argument that it would be better to teach her daughter now than to have to fix her later. The woman nodded, saying something like, "Okay, I will take your money, and you better not be smoking around the girl." Brendan liked the vocal instructor who was as gentle with her new student as she was outspoken with Brendan.

A shiver in the nearby brittlebush caught Brendan's attention through her peripheral vision. Brendan held her breath and turned her head slowly. A couple inches from her face was a lizard, a zebra-tail with its striped appendage curling toward the sky. It was too dark out to see if the creature's skin was splashed with the lemon and orange hues that appeared during breeding season. She imagined the lizard as a neon sign, something she had not seen in half a decade, not since the earthquake.

Beyond that, however, she realized what had caused the lizard to run, to offer its regenerative tail up as if-needed consolation bait. Fuck, Brendan mouthed, then immediately hoped she had not said it aloud. She could not make out exactly who it was. She could not tell if it was a colleague. Brendan had been expecting a visit from the program. Although her field work was immaculate, she was a year overdue for a medical exam.

Brendan played dead. Without moving her mouth, she took slow and shallow breaths, ones that would not be detected beneath the batting of her sleeping bag. Moreover, she willed her eyelids not to blink. As the man approached, slowly, lowering his headlamp to keep it angled down and toward Brendan's body, she could see that he was holding a gun. It almost shimmered in the lamplight.

Upon reaching her, the man took one hand off the gun. He stretched his arm out, slowly, to check for a pulse. Although blinded by the artificial light, the moment that Brendan felt the man's fingers against her neck, she thrust her forearms forward. The quick-release zipper on her sleeping bag gave way. Brendan grabbed the barrel of the gun with one hand and the grip with the other, making sure to come in from above in a quick and deliberate motion, snapping the man's wrist downward, freeing the weapon from his control. In a sweeping motion, Brendan slipped the man's other arm out from under him and rolled herself on top. Brendan hated guns. She was careful to keep her finger on the trigger guard, not the trigger.

Startled, the man did not move. Brendan hoped she had not hurt him. With one hand, she reached toward the man's forehead and palmed the headlamp, knowing the button would be either on the top or on the side. The light switched off. For a moment, both scientists held their breaths.

Brendan's eyes took a moment to adjust. The first thing that she could make out beneath that post-midnight sky was the faint silhouette of the man's bulky hearing protection. From the shape of the earmuffs, Brendan could tell that he was one of her colleagues. Beneath them, he also must have worn his company-issued, custom-molded earplugs, another piece of mandatory personal protective equipment. Still, the tunes of the whales were thunderous, deafening.

As Brendan set down the gun, her colleague's eyes widened. His body, which had just started to relax, re-stiffened. By pointing, emphatically, at his own headgear, the scientist asked, Where is your hearing protection?! Despite all the time alone that she had to think, Brendan was not sure how to answer.

Maddie was short for Madrigal, a name meaning "a song for many voices." The girl had been lost in the same unexpected earthquake that summoned these strange whales. For each sound that Brendan heard since the planet had swallowed her daughter, she felt that much further away. Brendan had known that, very soon, the memory of her daughter's voice would have been lost to her forever. In a way, through the silence, Brendan had stopped time. She looked toward the sky at the silent-to-her chorus of whlaes. She smiled for the first time in years.

Queen of the Machines

By Bob Dancer

It's 2002 and Shirley and I both receive monthly invitations for slot tournaments at the Golden Nugget, as well as from many other casinos. These Golden Nugget events go from Thursday midnight to early Sunday morning. We know most of the players, many of the employees, and each month it's worth an average of about $1,000 to us.

Apiece.

Of course, we sign up.

The one for May 2002 is going to end on the 12th, Mother's Day. I suggest we invite Shirley's mother, Virginia, to come with us. Virginia loves to gamble at video poker. Unfortunately, she has no skills at the game and regularly loses half of her Social Security check to the casinos. When she plays with me, which happens about once a month, she neither wins nor loses money at gambling, but she gets to play, eat well, and spend time with people who love her. And when she returns home afterward, she takes with her a variety of gift cards for things such as gasoline, restaurants, grocery stores, and Walmart.

Virginia prefers cash, of course, but cash tends to slip through her fingers. More than once we gave her $500 when she left us, and she immediately went to a casino and didn't leave until the money was all gone. So, we rarely give her cash anymore. Periodically we take her car to a mechanic we trust who tells us what the car needs to run reliably, and we pay to have it done. And sometimes Virginia brings her prescriptions with her and Shirley gets them filled. We aren't stingy with her, but believe she gets a lot more value out of what we give her if it isn't actual money.

Virginia lives about 100 miles south of us, near three different families she's related to— two daughters and one grown granddaughter, with young children in two of those families. None of those families has much of a financial cushion. But they still love to gamble! They live close to Laughlin, a casino town 90 miles south of Las Vegas.

We order a two-bedroom suite at the Golden Nugget so Virginia can both be with us and have a bit of privacy. On the morning of Thursday, May 9, before Virginia arrives to accompany us to the Golden Nugget, Shirley receives a call from a friend who tells her about a special women's religious seminar starting the next day. On Friday it's between 9 a.m. and 9 p.m., and Saturday it will go until 5 p.m. Shirley prefers to attend the conference much more than she wants to go to the casino. Shirley wants to know is this a problem for me, and can I please still take Virginia along?

This isn't a shock to me. Casinos are more my thing than Shirley's. And for the first seven years of our marriage, almost always when there was a good play at a casino, she was right there with me. Through some combination of skill and luck, we were able to strike it rich, relatively speaking. And if you can't do what you really want to do when you become relatively rich, what's the point?

So now when she asks, I usually agree to let her do something else. While we would have an extra $1,000 on average if Shirley participated in the tournament, this weekend it will just be Virginia and me. There will be an awards banquet starting at 6 p.m. Saturday, and Shirley promises to be there. And I know she won't back out of this one. After all, there will be a dance band and that's Shirley's favorite part of these events.

I really don't mind taking Virginia. Not too much. Except when I have to cut her off, which has happened a few times and wasn't fun for either one of us. But that hasn't happened recently and I'm optimistic I won't have to do it again. At least not this weekend. So, after she arrives, we leave Virginia's car in front of our house and take my car to the casino which is about 15 miles away.

Virginia will have no financial stake in the game. But she has a big emotional stake. She is disappointed when we lose, but figures I'm an expert and know what I'm doing. She's happy when we win. Especially, though, she's delighted that she just gets to play. Video poker is her favorite activity, but she doesn't have the funds or the knowledge to play it nearly as much as she would like.

Virginia and I eat at Stefano's Ristorante inside the Golden Nugget. When you're a big player, all the food and alcohol you want is free. Neither of us drink, but we really enjoy the food. It's so much better than the crap she eats at the Riverside Casino in Laughlin, which is where she usually goes when by herself or with one of her other daughters. And the waiters here singing Italian songs is a nice touch. I go over the ground rules for the weekend.

"I want to start playing at about 3 a.m. so I'm going

to want to go to bed after dinner. If you want to stay up more, I'll set you up with a movie on the TV in your room. And I brought along the latest Danielle Steel books-on-tape novel for you. Shirley keeps a list of the ones you've already listened to, and we're pretty sure you haven't heard this one.

"Shirley sent along some protein bars for the morning, and we'll get some water and coffee from the cocktail waitress at the machines. We'll eat breakfast three or four hours after we start playing. That sound all right?"

This is fine with Virginia. She's willing to agree to almost anything if she gets to play video poker.

I continue. "Remember, when it's your turn to play, after the deal and you make the play you think is right, you must wait until I okay your play or correct you. If you fail to do this, even once, you won't be able to play anymore." She could play by herself with her own money, of course, except she doesn't have any.

Virginia nods. She accepts that I'm really firm about this. It isn't that she's a terrible player. She's not. She gets most of the plays correct. But getting most right isn't nearly good enough. We are going to be playing a $25 machine, which means $125 every hand. Unsupervised, Virginia would make more than $1,000 worth of mistakes every hour on a game that big. No thanks. We have a pretty big edge when I'm calling the shots, almost $200 an hour on average, but Virginia's non-expertise could crush that edge and turn us into a big loser.

"I will go slow and wait for you," she promises. "Playing on a machine that big is exciting. It's like I died and have gone to heaven."

My alarm goes off at 2:30 a.m. I knock on her door, stick my head in far enough so she can hear me and say, "Twenty-five minutes. She mumbles some undecipherable response. I go back into my room to stretch, shower, shave, and otherwise get ready. She pops out of her bedroom into the common area of our suite at 2:55. We go downstairs.

Both of the two $25 machines I want are available, while all of the $5 machines are busy, even at 3 in the morning. While the bigger machines are worth more on average, you also lose more on them when you don't win. It's a very good play over time, but you have no idea what's going to happen this weekend. You need more than a half-million-dollar gambling bankroll to handle the swings on that machine comfortably. Most players don't have that, and some of the ones that have the money can't psychologically handle losing $30,000 or more in one day. So, these machines are usually available when I want them. We won't gamble on both machines, but they are side by side and it allows us both to sit together without inconveniencing anybody else.

Before we begin to play, I call the slot shift boss over. He recognizes me, of course, and would have recognized Shirley, too, but he has never seen Virginia before. I introduce her as Shirley's mother and explain that we'll be playing together with my money. Regardless of whoever is sitting down when a jackpot is hit, the tax form is to be made out in my name and I'm the one to be paid. He verifies with Virginia that all jackpots go to me and she nods. Since we are both in agreement on this, it's a no-brainer to him.

Technically he doesn't have to agree to this, and at many casinos they don't. Officially, whoever hits the button that leads to a jackpot owns the jackpot. But Shirley and I are regulars and, in his mind, I'm being a good son-in-law. So sure. He has no problem with this.

We sit down to play. Ladies first. We agree to switch every 15 minutes, or when we get a 4-of-a-kind or bigger, whichever comes first. The machine locks up on these 4-of-a-kind jackpots (worth $3,125) and I'll need to sign for a tax form before we get paid and are allowed to continue. She plays slowly and waits for me to either correct her or to say she got it right.

It isn't that the game we're playing, Jacks or Better, is particularly difficult. It's not. It's arguably the easiest video poker game around. But at each casino I've played with Virginia, we play a different game. Sometimes the game to play is Double Bonus, sometimes Double Double Bonus, other times Deuces Wild. Each of these games has a different strategy. While keeping the games straight is part of being a professional, and second nature to me now, Virginia plays all games more or less the same. I explain the differences each time, but she's 74 years old and doesn't remember these things very well. With every hand I have to watch her very closely.

Periodically friends come by to say "Hi." They are a little bit surprised that Shirley isn't there, but I explain that Virginia is Shirley's mother and Shirley asked her to come along and babysit me this weekend. They smile at my stupid little joke. Some of them tease me and tell Virginia that she'll have to watch me very closely because I'm such a naughty little boy. And we smile back.

When it's my turn to play, I play faster than she does. But not as fast as I can. If I come across a good teaching point, I'll explain to Virginia why I make one hold rather than another. She actually enjoys learning about the distinctions, but she won't remember them.

About two hours into our play, Virginia holds the jack of clubs by itself. I tell her okay, and she draws four perfect cards. The ace of clubs, king of clubs, queen of clubs, and the ten of clubs. A royal flush.

A $100,000 royal flush!

Drawing four perfect cards is a very rare achievement. And yet it happens sometimes. When you least expect it.

Many people get wild and crazy when they hit a big jackpot. Virginia just sits there stupefied. She looks at me with her eyes wide open. I whisper quietly, "You did it!" For a while, she seems to struggle with her breathing a bit, but she's fine.

Jackpots this size are pretty rare in this casino. When the word gets out, many people come over to congratulate me, and I tell them that Virginia hit it. And so, they love on her. Tell her what a tremendous accomplishment it is. Tell her they've never hit one that big and it must be very exciting.

Virginia says "Yes, it is." The biggest one she's hit before this was for $4,000. And there's only been one of those. This is beyond her wildest dreams. She's going to be talking about this one for a long time, even though she doesn't get to keep the money.

I tell the employees that I'd like a check rather than cash. It takes a while for this to be accomplished. Large jackpots require the machine to be opened up and the innards checked to verify that no one has doctored the machine. This is always a tense time for me. I know I didn't do anything improper, but I cannot possibly know what anyone else has done to that machine before I got there. Fortunately everything checks out and we get paid.

Virginia stands up and is walking in a daze. I suggest that now is a good time for breakfast. We'll continue our play after we've eaten. We ask that the machine be locked up for us while we eat. No problem. The casino is happy to provide this service in hopes that we give back what we've just won.

After breakfast, it's about 6:30 in the morning. I suggest we call Shirley. I don't know what time she's planning on getting up for her church seminar, but I can't imagine she'll object too much to this phone call. She picks up the phone with a "What's wrong?" I tell her nothing bad has happened, but Virginia has something to tell her. Virginia starts crying and tells Shirley she hit a $100,000 royal flush. She never thought she'd do that in her lifetime. Even though the money belongs to Shirley and me and not Virginia, she couldn't be happier. Shirley screams for joy while Virginia cries. She says she'll see us tomorrow night.

We return to the machine and continue our play. We lose a bit, which is normal. Usually in video poker you gradually go down, down, down between big jackpots. This happens to everyone. If you're playing the game successfully, you make more when you hit the big jackpots than you lose between jackpots.

For the slot tournament itself, it's just hit, hit, hit the button as fast as you can and hope for the best. Virginia does the honors. As near as I can tell, it's almost all luck. Between Shirley and me together, we make it into the top ten (worth between $1,000 and $10,000) at the Golden Nugget events about once a year. Not this time though. A bit disappointing, but not a surprise.

At the awards banquet, Shirley's a bit late because her seminar ran long. But Virginia and I hold a seat for her. When Shirley comes in, she wants to dance immediately. That's Shirley! While we do a West Coast Swing to "Mustang Sally," we notice several people come over and talk to Virginia. Congratulating her, I suppose. After all, a $100,000 jackpot is the stuff that many players dream about.

We dance several more times that evening, and players keep coming up to Virginia. When I ask her about it, she said many of them were wishing her a happy Mother's Day.

Many of the players are about Shirley's and my age, and we're in our early 50s. Many of them no longer have a mother around. And the ones that do still have a mother realize that they've chosen to spend Mother's Day in a casino rather than visiting with dear old mom. Somehow, it seems like wishing Virginia a happy Mother's Day kind of makes up for, well, not spending a moment to wish it to their own mothers.

Sometimes, any old mother will do!

A Betting Chance

By Tonya Todd

Sasha stripped down to her seamless red thong and stared at the array of clothing covering her bed. She couldn't even choose a bra before knowing what blouse she'd wear.

Scrutinizing the selection, her cat padded between the items lining her quilt. He swished his fluffy grey tail with disapproval. Either he wanted a spot for his early evening nap, or he didn't like the selections any better than she did.

"Not now, Bennet." She lifted him and set him on the floor. "The last thing I need is cat hair on everything."

Only thirty minutes remained before Luke's expected arrival. Sasha ransacked the piles for the right combination and donned her twelfth potential outfit for the night.

She checked the mirror. "Ugh." Still not right. She tossed them back on the bed.

Slacks were essential. Anything else might mislead her date. Make him think they could be more than friends.

Make her lose the bet.

Smearing almond oil over her legs, she returned their ashy hue to smooth tawny and scanned her choices again. Nothing. Nothing would work. If she didn't choose something soon, she'd still be naked when Luke arrived.

Three hard knocks bellowed from her front door. Bennet ran from the room. Sasha covered her breasts. She wasn't ready for any of this. It was too soon.

She snagged a silk robe from its hook. The cool material, as she wrapped it around her bare skin, soothed her heated frenzy.

Just because he'd shown up half an hour early, didn't mean she should rush. Let him pay the price for not getting there on time. With calm determination, she sauntered out of her room and to the front door.

Despite her bold stance, relief washed over her when she checked the peephole. Instead of Luke's ghostlike beauty, a brawny bronze angel waited on the other side. She was saved.

With Jacob's help, she'd definitely find an outfit to send the right message. No more fear of mixed signals.

She threw open the door to welcome her friend.

Jacob swept in with a flourish. "Find something to wow him yet?"

That was the whole reason she needed him. The clothes on her bed weren't nice enough for dinner, but if she wore something appropriate, something that hinted at possible investment, Luke might mistake her decorum as interest.

One brow arched, Jacob primped her curls. With a salacious smile, he assessed her current state of undress. "That'll do it."

"No one's wowing anyone." She tightened the belt on her silk robe. "I plan to appease my misguided suitor by going through the motions and fulfilling my perfunctory role as mechanically as possible to prove the fruitlessness of our pairing. That is all."

"Girl, you trippin'." Jacob spun her around and nudged her toward the bedroom. "Get in there, and let's get you ready."

But she would never be ready for Luke. Not really. The man had stepped out of a Jane Austen novel to sweep her off her feet. If her four decades taught her anything, it was that the Wickhams of the world favored the pleasures found in Las Vegas, not a true Mr. Darcy.

And as a separated mother of three, she was no Elizabeth.

Jacob shook his head at the chaos on her bed. "You aren't even trying."

Given that the contrived date simulation served only to placate a curiosity and fulfill the terms of her first bet with Jacob, what she wore didn't matter. Not really. She held up pant No. 2 with shirt No. 9, crisp black slacks with a blue button-down blouse. "How about this?"

"Sweetie." He rubbed his temples as though massaging away her painful suggestion. "It's not a job interview."

"Well, it's not a real date either." On a real date, she would already know what to wear, not to mention, where they were eating that evening. In fact, she would probably have planned the whole thing, controlling the night instead of leaving her fate to a random crapshoot.

"Be honest," Jacob said. "How much of this is you trying to win the new bet versus freaking out because you really like him?"

"I don't— I just—" Her words sputtered.

Any handsome man might engage the eye, but Luke aroused her mind. All the more challenging to resist.

Her tingling tongue triggered a minty memory. The cool tickle of his breath. The fresh spark in his fire-blue eyes. The firm press of his lips when, during their drama class performance, "Drake and Lily's Break-up" morphed into a public declaration of Luke's interest in more than friendship.

Okay, maybe she sort of liked him. And maybe there was some part of her that wished she wasn't damaged goods. But she didn't have the bandwidth to start dating again. Couldn't spare the time from her acting career.

Besides, Sin City was no place to fall in love. Las Vegas meant bright lights, big city. She'd rather take the stage and risk tomatoes than roll the dice with her heart.

Losing the first bet may have forced her into this experiment, but failing again meant agreeing to a second date. Extra bet or not, a second date might lead to a third. And third dates ...

No. This ended *tonight*.

A warm hand on her elbow tugged her back to awareness. Jacob offered a gentle squeeze. "If I send you out like this, I may as well forfeit. He'll never try to kiss you again."

"Works for me." It would certainly make all this easier.

"Well, it doesn't work for our bet." He set his hands on his hips. "You promised you'd try."

That was when she thought she'd win the first bet.

"Fine." She could still express platonic intentions draped in a plain frock. Something simple and boring that deemphasized her curves. "Let's look through my closet."

He followed her into the walk-in wardrobe and

scooped an armful of silk and satin gowns. "Now we're talking." He headed toward the door, then broke to an abrupt halt. "What's with all this blank space? I can't believe you haven't taken over the whole closet yet."

"It hasn't been that long." Five weeks to the day.

Not that she was counting anniversaries anymore.

Jacob spread her dresses out to breathe on an abandoned rod. "The space is yours now. Use it."

Together they perused the buffet of options. A peach shirtdress. A tangerine shift. A watermelon mini. She pointed to a plum maxi that dangled shapeless from its hanger.

"You've got to be kidding." He dismissed her suggestion with a wave and lifted her spearmint halter dress from the rod. "This one. It's hot without trying."

"I can't wear that."

"Why not?"

Besides the fact that she wasn't aiming for hot, Luke had admired that dress during their first interaction, when she was still trying to set him up with Jacob. Boy, had she misread that encounter. She never would have agreed to a jaunt around Sunset Park quoting Shakespeare on Luke's arm had she known he was straight. "He's already seen me in it."

"Gone." Jacob thrust it back to the rod. He flipped through more options, then paused at a cherry-red gown. "Try this."

Sasha caressed the smooth satin and fingered the velvet lace. The last time she'd worn this curve-hugging, flowy number was at the only Las Vegas performance of *Alice Through the Looking Glass*. When gliding across the Smith Center's grey marble tiles, she embraced the palatial opulence of salmon-stoned walls, teardrop light fixtures hanging from sky-high ceilings, and the bronze *Genius in Flight* statue. Emboldened with the power only such a gown can provide, she'd aimed to strut the aisle to her center seat with the same grace and elegance as the Red Queen.

Tonight's affair must not involve that type of magic. Not if she planned to prevent a goodnight kiss. Even if she phoned in the entire evening to win the bet, the allure of this dress could blow her blasé performance. As he walked her to the door, Luke might be tempted to fan her skirt with a twirl, then whirl her into his arms for one glorious smooch.

Heat flushed over Sasha's face and neck. "You're trying to sabotage me."

"Look." A knowing grin eased across Jacob's face. "If you could dress yourself, you wouldn't have to worry about my motives."

"That wasn't a denial."

"Oh, girl." He dabbed the faux sweat from his brow.

"I'm so glad you brought up denial. Can we dish about the real reason you'll lose tonight's bet?"

Sasha's mouth fell open, but resisted a verbal response. A yes or no would admit her expected defeat. Anything more would invite a tea party with unwanted spills.

Her buzzing phone saved her from responding. Without apology, she slipped back into her bedroom, grabbed her cell from the dresser, and checked her notifications. A text from Luke.

–Identify the quote: Sentence first, verdict afterward.

Sasha squeezed her phone. It was bad enough he'd hijacked her evening. Couldn't he wait until they were together before stimulating her brain? Her phone buzzed again.

–Stump you already?

Ferocious fingers typed her response.

–Stuff and nonsense!

He'd need more than Lewis Carroll to challenge her. Especially with her Smith Center experience fresh on her mind.

She chewed her lip, meditating on the coincidence. Others might read some type of sign into it. For her, it only proved why they'd make great friends.

"Hello, queen." Jacob bounded from the closet holding up a black satin gown in one hand, two matching opera gloves in the other. "Why come to play when you can slay?"

"That's tempting." If she were attending a coronation. "Let's lose the gl—"

The doorbell rang. They shared a panicked look.

"I'm late," she said. "I'm late!"

"For a very important—"

"Don't." She stabbed her finger at him, daring him to continue.

He beamed at the black gown. "Guess you have to wear this."

Calming herself with a deep breath, she extricated the satin ensemble from his grip. "Let him in. I'll get dressed."

Once alone with her selections, Sasha worked through her options again. If Luke liked her as much as Jacob claimed, he'd try to kiss her no matter what she wore. But even if the odds weren't in her favor, she was in the right city to beat them.

Except that the house always wins.

Rather than fold her cards, it was time to assume the position of power. Put him on the defense. She touched up her hair and makeup, then changed into her final outfit.

When Sasha stepped out from the hall, she sashayed toward Luke with purpose. Despite the extra inches her heels provided, he stood taller than she remembered. His snug, cobalt button-down, sleeves tucked at the elbow, augmented the blue in his eyes. His jackpot smile lit the room.

"That dress." He glided forward two quick steps, then broke to a forceful stop. "It's …"

She withheld a satisfied smile. Not only did this dress paint her in an intimidating light, it matched her favorite bold lipstick. No more running from Luke's chase. Her imperious presence would dissuade his approach.

His shoulders relaxed, and he recovered his usual poise. Stepping closer, he presented a crimson Stargazer lily. "Red is your color."

She half-expected roses, but Luke wasn't much for clichés. Even beautiful ones.

Noting his slick, obsidian curls, perfectly gelled into place save one over his right brow, she restrained the urge to brush them into place. "Because I'm angry and aggressive?" Or was it her burning cheeks?

"You're passionate." He pushed closer, backing her to the wall, then brushed the velvet petals over her cheek. "And driven."

Sasha's heart pounded. Already he called her power bluff. Careful to avoid grazing his flesh, she peered into his eyes and wrapped her fingers around his offering. She breathed in the floral bouquet, reflecting on his opening act and his too-attractive appearance. The kind of sexy that would make a weaker woman reconsider.

Safe behind the flower, she reminded herself of the risk. Only pain could result from involvement. Now was not the time to gamble on romance.

"I'll take that." Jacob popped up from out of nowhere and reached for the lily.

She double-blinked, having forgotten he was there.

Leaning in, he whispered, "You're going down."

Reluctantly releasing the flower barrier, she raised her chin to resume her stately manner. "Excuse us a moment."

"By all means." Luke's eyes twinkled with sincerity. As she stepped away, he caught her wrist. "Take all the time you need."

Electricity surged, branding the moment with their brief touch. Sasha pulled her gaze from him and escaped to her kitchen.

Snickering more with every step, Jacob followed close behind her. "New bet. Double or nothing."

She wouldn't let him intimidate her. Not in her Queen of Hearts dress. "Already scared to lose?"

Jacob guffawed. "Ten seconds together and he pinned you against the wall. Tonight's kiss is a forgone conclusion."

"I wasn't ..." She swallowed, stifling the image of

Luke pressing her to the paint. She shook out her wrist. "It wasn't that close."

"Please, if I hadn't interrupted, you'd be sucking face right now." Jacob twisted his lips, clearly restraining some pressing point. "This bet is too easy. The stakes are too low. When he kisses you goodnight, all you have to do is agree to a second date."

"Assuming he asks."

"He will."

"And assuming he doesn't turn out to be a huge jerk."

"Obviously."

"Fine." She tapped a red sole on the tile. There was no way to double her loss. Luke couldn't kiss her goodnight twice. She fingered her bottom lip. Even if he did, extra kisses wouldn't mean additional dates. "Continue."

"No need to go all salty Sasha on me." Jacob threw his neck into it for emphasis. "I notice you didn't question whether or not he'll kiss you."

Her jaw sealed shut. He was right. Some part of her must have already accepted defeat. And attempting to lie couldn't overcome it. "What's the new bet?"

"The goodnight bet is still on. But ..." Jacob bounced in place, far too giddy about his proposal. "If he kisses you before that, you have to be the one to ask him out."

"But that will make him think ..."

"Uh-huh." Jacob nodded.

"And then he'll expect—"

"—You to give him more than a rigged free spin." He bopped her nose with the lily.

"Stop being vulgar." Though not opposed to thwarting gender norms, extending invitations didn't make sense. Not when actively avoiding a relationship.

"It's not vulgar," he said. "Free spins never win. They offer false hope, which isn't really fair."

She hadn't thought about that. Sure, she'd been up front with Luke about her hesitation. Like a gentleman, he promised not to push. To go at any pace she desired, if she'd at least try.

But she didn't try. And she wouldn't be pretending to try now, if not for losing last week's bet to Jacob.

"And you have to wear the black satin number, gloves and all." Jacob, who instead of charging in as her trusty knave, arrived as more of a wild card.

All he earned from these stupid bets were bragging rights and watching her squirm. She's the one who got to spend time with Luke. It might feel like a reward if not for the inevitable heartbreak.

The hollow wound in her chest ached. So far she'd only rolled snake eyes on love. Only a fool would ante up again.

"Sweetie." Jacob brushed a spiral of curls behind her

ear. "You have got to work on your poker face."

She searched his eyes, trying to read his. "Why is this so important to you?"

He looped his arm in hers and pointed her toward the living room. "Look at this man."

Studying her family photos with interest, Luke scratched Bennet's ears while cradling him in his arms. Her age didn't bother this man. Nor did her children. He wasn't even concerned about cat fur.

Jacob's warm hand caressed her shoulder. "If a guy like Luke can't get you to try again, you might never move your clothes to the rest of the closet."

"Okay," she whispered. "I accept your new terms."

"And the dress?"

"The gown. The gloves. Everything."

Jacob danced a victory waltz with her flower.

"But..." She plucked the lily from him.

Luke turned toward the commotion and returned Bennet to the floor. Arm outstretched, he reached a hand for Sasha. "Shall we?"

Inhaling the lily's essence to resist the magnetic pull, she eyed Luke through the petals. "If I win, you go six months without meddling in my love life."

"With all that heat," said Jacob, "I won't have to."

Sasha handed over the lily. She fixed her gaze on Luke. No more fighting him either. Gravitating toward him, she stepped into his orbit and accepted his hand.

For the rest of the night, all bets were off.

Graveyard

By Mauricio Ortiz Zaragoza

When I started working for my dad's janitorial business straight out of high school, it was supposed to be
a temporary gig. Make a little money on the side while
I went to school during the week, get my feet wet with
some job experience, and help my father out in the
meantime.

I ended up doing it for almost a decade, a third of
my life gone by at the same position with little to show
for it besides the constant feeling that I had wasted the
best years of my life. The work was easy and the pay
was good. At 22, $16 an hour seemed fair for the grave-
yard shift, and I didn't have a social life to spend any
money on. Along with nearly every employee, I worked

exclusively at night during both weekdays and weekends, depending on whatever store with which we had contracted. The hours gave me plenty of time to think about things. The store managers would lock us in for the shift and return the next morning. Voluntary incarceration with pay.

My father made it sound like a sweet deal, an exciting opportunity for a father-son business. He and my mother called me into his home office the day after I graduated. We talked about my future as I sat on the same couch where me and my brother played our Gameboy Colors when Ma had to work as a housekeeper at the Bellagio. We would be there all day as he scheduled crews and fielded calls from angry store managers, many of them turning into shouting matches about missing coats of wax or about workers who showed up late. I thought about how much and how little had changed, hoping I could make up something vague I could finesse on the spot.

My dad spoke first. "So now that you've finished school, what's next? College or work? We're expanding into more stores and I want to know if you're interested in helping me by working nights."

"Well, I'm thinking about going to film school, maybe applying to UCLA since it's only a few hours away. Mr. Mac and all of my classmates really liked the videos I made for his broadcasting class, and it's something I want to take further."

"We want you to go for your dreams," my mom said in her best English before switching over to Spanish. "But your dad wants you to have something to fall back on in case something happens. I wanted to be an architect like your grandfather before he died. I had to quit school to take care of my mom and my sisters and I don't want you to have nothing.

My dad nodded in agreement. "I need people I can trust to take my business to the next level and I want you with me. If you like the business, you could even run it someday and hand it over to one of your sons."

I looked over al all the model airplanes and Thunderbirds memorabilia that littered his office. More remnants of his days as a pilot before his own father refused to pay for aviation school. "Yeah, Dad, I'd love to help out however I can." He sold me on working from 9 to 5 nightly by making it sound like I was doing him a favor.

But there's only so much late-night brooding that's possible working with the same cleaning crew on a regular basis. I got to know a few of my co-workers in rotation well enough over the years. Some of them, I could tell, thought getting close to the boss's kid couldn't hurt their careers, so they'd try to strike up conversation and get friendly with me. The family business was competitive against others in acquiring contracts, because many of the workers were undocumented. Almost all of them were Latino men, immigrants who came north to wax floors and scrub toilets to make a living for themselves or to send money back home. I wondered if there was resentment between us when they'd point out how easily I could pass for white, since I had light skin and shortened my given name, Gustavo, to just Gus. None of them were close to my age and their English was as good as my Spanish—*más o menos*. But language is never a barrier when you're talking *about* women and drinking, which they zeroed in on as what men their age were supposed to talk about with someone like me.

"Oyé, Gustavo," they'd ask me on a regular basis in Spanish. "How many girls you bang this weekend?"

"*Muchas*" was my go-to reply in Spanglish. "*Muchas chicas bonitas.*"

I ran through plenty of these self-deprecating jokes, because it was embarrassing to admit that girls my age never paid much attention to me romantically, seeing me as either "safe" or not in that light at all. Not that I'm complaining. But that lack of experience made my first romantic interaction rather eventful.

I was alone on the Strip late one summer night, and it was closer to dawn than midnight as I was heading to my car from a friend's get-together at the Flamingo.

I had never been out on the Strip this late as an adult, so I walked it up and down trying to work off the rum and Cokes in my system before driving home. As I went down Las Vegas Boulevard, seeing it emptier than I'd ever seen it before, a woman going the other direction stopped me. She pointed out a "Feel the Bern" sticker I still had on my jacket from the Nevada Caucus earlier that month.

"Hey, I really like your sticker," she said. "I think Bernie's really for the people, you know?"

"Oh yeah, me too."

"So listen—" she said, putting her hand on my shoulder. "Do you want a massage?"

"At this hour?" Then I knew what she was asking me. "Uh, actually I'm not staying on the Strip, because I live here, so I don't have a—"

Before I could finish explaining, she said "Oh" and walked away. Just like that. She propositioned me and moved on to the next one without missing a beat.

What a city to live in, I thought, wondering what else I was missing out on as I realized this kind-faced stranger in the middle of the night would be the first woman to ever hit on me. Maybe now I had something to share whenever somebody asked me about the women in my life, although I wasn't sure how to feel about it.

I told Christian, a middle-aged Mexican guy from the

crew I was closest to, about it when we were stripping floors together to see if what happened that night was anything out of the ordinary.

"Nah, man. I felt weird about paying for it before I finally did. Don't feel bad about those kinds of girls, because everybody pays for it in the end. There's nothing wrong with a man who doesn't want to deal with all that bullshit just to get some, so don't worry about it."

Decent guys, but definitely products of their time. Patronizing sex work wasn't up my alley for other reasons, but I was drawn in by the allure of encounters like that, the anything-goes vibe of Las Vegas. Love is for sale by the hour and there's no last call, except for downtown—thanks, but no thanks.

I told myself that roaming around the margins of the city and its dive bars would give me the right sort of eyes for the stories I was working on at night. Everything I wrote during those late hours locked up somewhere sounded phony to me: hand-me-down experiences from movies and anecdotes that never went anywhere. My dad said I was "book smart," but not "street smart," and only one of those would protect you from getting taken advantage of. What I needed in my life was out there, waiting for someone like me to bear witness to all the has-beens and the ones who never had a chance. Who knows, maybe that special someone might be out there while I was stuck mopping floors and dreaming about how different things could have been.

One of them did, and I pushed her out at the first sign of trouble. Laurie was a high school friend and the closest thing I had to a real relationship. There was something there, and I could see it in the way she looked at me and how it made me feel. But I wasn't ready for the kind of love and commitment that I knew was possible with her. Just making eye contact with her filled me with nausea, the kind that keeps you from functioning, because you're so worried about how wrecked you're going to be when it comes to a crashing halt. We had a good thing going, and it felt like she was ruining it by developing strong feelings, wanting more than I could give anyone.

She was my first everything and I broke her heart before she could do the same to me. It seemed like the least shitty thing to do. Like ripping off a bandage so we could both move on with our lives. I was trying not to think about her the next time I went out drinking, but it couldn't be helped. Me and Christian hit the PT's down the street after the job, trying to get a head start on a three-day weekend. I didn't sleep the day before—too many stimulants in my system to get through finals, personal turmoil, and an overnight shift to top it off. One or all of those handicaps started me on Laurie, openly wondering in a dead-empty bar at eight o'clock in the morning if I had made the wrong call for the right reasons, or just another excuse to feel sorry. Christian may have been giving me the benefit of the doubt when he put his hand on my shoulder and ordered two shots of hornitos.

"I'm gonna give you some advice I wish I had when I was your age," he said, downing the shot before signaling the bartender for another. "Never sweat pussy. Ever. Life's too short to be crying in your beer and playing sad shit on the jukebox because of a woman."

"I'll drink to that," I said, not knowing how else to reply.

I thought about his remark and all it could have meant when I first noticed Faye noticing me. Or maybe I just imagined that in retrospect. She may have been my best friend's girlfriend, but that always made her more attractive to me when I wondered what she was doing with Alex in the first place. He was aspiring to everything, but working toward none of it, content to pick up dogshit for the rest of his life for minimum wage while his employer stiffed him on everything. We were best friends by default, because everybody else in our friend group had left town and we lived down the street from each other. Toward the end of our friendship, I found myself hanging around them, because Faye was more interesting and alive than he had ever been. They were ill-suited for each other and as their relationship deteriorated, I was there for all the shit-talking and complaints he had about her, all of it lowering my opinion of him. He confided in me that this was the fifth girlfriend in a row to have cheated on him. None of them were his fault, just like nothing in his life was.

I didn't feel any loyalty for Alex when she invited me over, months after they had broken up. As Faye took me into her room, I couldn't think of a good reason why I shouldn't go along with whatever ended up happening between us, even if I felt sick to my stomach the moment I saw her again. When we got there, she immediately went into her closet and took out a caged bra, a wired bra with straps all over that looked faintly like something in the leather/BDSM section of a sex store.

"This," she said "is why he broke up with me and said I cheated on him." She held it in front of her chest and then wore it over her shirt. "This is the 'lingerie' I supposedly bought that he never saw. He threw all of my shit in the trash—my drawings, my extra glasses, my cat's toys—because of this. Does this look like fucking lingerie to you?"

"Not really. He's always been passive-aggressive, so jumping to conclusions sounds like him. But that's ... well, a different level of messed up. I'm sorry you had to go through that."

I hadn't been expecting to find out what really happened between them when I came over, but we ended up talking about it for at least an hour. When the atmosphere turned lighter and away from memories neither one of us wanted to drag on any further, we drank Jameson straight from her flask. She lit up a pre-rolled joint and when she handed it to me, I felt that cross-fade hit hard, making me cough and lose any semblance of self-control I had going in. All I could think about was her inching closer to me, putting her hand on my knee as I tried to steady myself and decide whether or not to stop this. She went for it, a quick kiss, and immediately apologized while I focused on keeping the room from spinning. Something in my head told me I'd spend the rest of my life regretting either option in this situation, so I went with the one that made me feel warmer, and closer to someone I had wanted so badly for so long.

That night was Sunday going into Monday morning. We both had work a full 24 hours later, since Faye worked 9 to 5 at the animal hospital. When we woke up around midnight, I was the one to suggest hitting happy hour at Stake Out Bar & Grill, hoping some familiar faces and cheap beer would ease my anxiety about the next move going forward. As we pulled in, I parked next to a white Ford Raptor in front of the bar.

I pointed it out to Faye. "My dad drives a Ford truck just like that one."

Wonder how many of those you see around a place like this, I thought as we walked in, sat at the bar, and ordered two shots of Jameson and two chaser PBRs.

"Cheers," I said and after taking that shot, I looked over to the other side of the bar. A man was standing up behind his stool, his back turned to us next to a woman who looked ten years younger than him. I recognized my father by his gray, receding hair and short, stocky build.

"We gotta go *now*," I said, grabbing her arm and ushering her out as she tried to ask why.

We were out the door and in my car when Faye said, "Wait, what about the drinks?"

"Forget the drinks," I muttered. I debated sending her in with cash to pay for the drinks, but that didn't feel right. None of this did.

I thought about the worst that could happen, only knowing that if worse came to worst, there would be no hesitation about what to do. Letting him walk from this wasn't an option.

"I'll be right back," I said, and walked in again.

When I did, I caught a glimpse of him walking up to the pool tables upstairs. *I'm not going to go up there and confront him,* I thought. *I'll just pay for the drinks and get home.*

I was standing at the bar trying to get the bartender's attention when I heard those loud crashes upstairs, the sound of a pool cue broken in half then thrown at the wall. I put down a $20 bill underneath the empty shot glass and walked out.

Faye asked me what was wrong again when I started the engine.

"Nothing."

She stopped trying to speak to me as I cranked the radio up and focused on nothing else but the road in front of me, trying my best not to swerve and to tell the color of the lights apart. When we got to her place, she tried one last time to reach me and switched the radio off.

"I know you're not okay. But I'm here if you need to talk about anything. At all."

I let a moment pass. "Please just go and leave me alone."

And she did.

I drove straight home.

I got home late before my father did. I was lying in bed, trying not to think about anything that had happened, when he showed up in my doorway.

"Hey, Gustavo, are you awake?"

"Yeah."

"I just came to say good night. Everything good?"

"Yeah, dad, yeah. Good night."

"Good night."

I slept in until four in the afternoon, a few hours before I had to go in to work. I didn't want to be at home until then, so I went to 7-Eleven to get coffee and drove to the place on Sunset and Eastern where you can park and watch the planes fly in and out of McCarran. Watching them, I thought about my earliest childhood memory, being 4 years old and flying into the United States from Mexico for the first and last time. I remembered looking at the Strip from the window, my dad holding me in his lap and pointing it out to me.

I finished my coffee and left for the clothing store where we had a deep scrub scheduled. When I got to the parking lot, I saw Christian outside of his car, on his phone and smoking a cigarette. He looked up, smiled, and said: "Hey, Gustavo, did you bang any hot chicks this weekend?"

"*Muchas*," I said. "*Muchas chicas bonitas.*"

Marshmallows and Butterflies

By Jen Nails

every city has a soul
every city is alive
we are as much a living, breathing entity
as you humans are

I am the desert
this valley
I'm sandstone and Calico Basin
layers of history
silver and gypsum

I'm the miners
the Mormons
the lost city of St. Thomas
Lake Mead

I'm a wisp
a spirit
a scorpion's night hunt
the thrumming of a Costa's hummingbird
burros and bighorn sheep

I'm every moment someone bets
every button pressed
lever pulled
cards laid
I'm poker rooms
the Moulin Rouge de Paris
Circus Vargas and Siegfried and Roy

I'm Luv-it Frozen Custard
every high school dance
all the strip malls
the 7th Street painted walls

I'm gallons of alcohol
and all the vices mixed
into one destination cocktail
I'm choices
impulses
vulnerability
secrets

I'm prayers
sent up for forgiveness
a pink sunset
and the orangest, swollen moon

I'm the Fremont Street Experience and the Strip
build a hitch-hiking cowboy!
tear down the hitch-hiking cowboy
build a theme park!
tear down the theme park
build a pirate ship!
tear down the pirate ship

I'm
constantly
destroying
and regenerating,
advertising
and inviting

each floor strung with dynamite
windows shattered
cranes and pollution
dust and debris
bigger and better

I eat the tourists
I bite into the skyline
like a rattlesnake to a hiker's ankle
bite into history
spit out tomorrow
revising
staying current
staying hot

I'm you
who live here
who work for pennies
or millions
or somewhere in between

you
holding this book in your hands
playing Scrabble in the courtyard
taking out the trash at the apartments
counting rests, on stage, French horn on your thigh
I'm the locals
the cogs and the wheels
the roots
We
Are
This
City

We're more than the pyramid,
than the roller coasters,
than the praying mantis and the stadium
more than what they see
when the pilot lowers the landing gear
We're the dirt underneath Cactus Joe's
we're aging in assisted-living homes
we're educating high school students
we're graduating, and off to college

Do you remember what they said about us
after gallons spilled
at Route 91
on October 1
after the terror on Las Vegas Boulevard
my heart
my soul
shattered
destroyed
prayers sent up

Do you remember that after that day
they couldn't believe
how compassionate Las Vegans were

Are

Couldn't believe that in
"a city like Las Vegas"
there could be a pause
an awareness
a collective grief

love
hovers
over the valley
I feel it every day

What follows are three moments
in three Las Vegas lives:
eggs hatching
chapters beginning
    keys modulating

They are dedicated to you
reader
Cheers
    to us
    to love
genuine love
between genuine people
"in a city like Las Vegas"

I want you to meet Moses Kaufman, 78 years old. It's December 2020. He's eating soup at Atria Sutton on Flamingo. They're calling it soup, but it's basically warm water and onion powder. Moses is losing his marbles (*his* prognosis). He isn't sure whether he is 17, in Denver, sitting in his old Ford, or if he's in his house on Oakey here in Las Vegas and the babies are sleeping, or if he's eating soup at Atria Sutton on Flamingo. He isn't sure if Helen is back at the room or if she's even alive or if she's in the house on Oakey.

He thinks it was in October that they played Scrabble in the courtyard. The next morning, she didn't wake up. Day after that, they buried her. No one was allowed at the service. He can see her fingers picking up each tile and placing it neatly in the bottom right corner and making B-I-R-D, triple word score, 21 points. He can smell the coffee on her lips. B-I-R-D one day. The next her lungs give out.

On this day, after his tray is left up on the counter, he makes his way down the hallway to Multi-Purpose Room A. There, a small woman sits in one of the big, burgundy armchairs.

"Comfy," she says, weaving her knitting needles through strings of yarn.

Moses nods. "These remind me of our living room," he says. He sits down in the one across from her.

"Living rooms," she says. "Did you do any living in yours?" She puts down her needles and quotes around the word "living" with her fingers. "Ours was so fancy. I was in my blue and mauve phase then, and the kids couldn't sit in there at all. We even had a piano. It only made noise when one of the cats jumped onto the keys and plink plink plink. But that wasn't music. Anyway. These chairs," she presses on the puffy armrest, "are marshmallows."

"Marshmallows," says Moses. "Mmmmm."

Marshmallows. And butterflies.

And clarity. Helen, his Helen, is gone.

Not gone to the bathroom, or gone to take a nap, or gone to book club.

Gone gone.

And he is capable of having butterflies?

"I'm ..." Moses says, and he closes his eyes, shifts in his chair, searching.

Nervous. All wires of emotion crossed, pushing at his sanity. This electric feeling toward this woman, the dread in his chest still fresh from Helen's death. He feels like he wants to tell the woman in the chair about the mornings he wakes up and is certain that he and Helen will have their coffee together, read the paper, take a walk, remind each other to take their pills. He *knows* that is what will happen. He can hear Helen's voice already, whispering, "Sleepyhead." He wants to tell this woman the crushing weight of the realization, almost every day since October, that she's gone. His best friend for 60 years. A limb amputated.

He squeezes his eyes shut tight, then opens them again. The woman's smiling at him. She's tiny and huge at the same time. One of those kinds of women that packs a punch.

"I'm ..." he tries again. Come on. His palms are wet. Finding the right words is like fishing for loose change in a pocket that got ripped from the back of your trousers years ago. And somehow, with the mask over his mouth, it's worse.

"I'm Rose," she says. "Who are you?"

"I'm Moses." Bingo. Thanks, Rose.

"Moses! From the Bible."

"That I am. I dropped those damn tablets."

She laughs. "You like tea?" she asks. "I'm making."

"No, I don't like tea. Never did. Brown water. Tea. I'm a coffee guy."

"Okay, Coffee Moses Guy. Suit yourself. But wait. Coffee's brown water, too."

"Coffee is not brown water."

"It is."

"It's not." Moses says. "Coffee is coffee. Tea is leaf-soaked water."

"Steeped," says Rose. "You steep to get tea. There's no soak." She quotes the word "soak" with her fingers.

"All right," Moses says, "I got my technique wrong. Still brown water, though."

"So is coffee."

Moses looks at Rose. Rose looks at Moses. They laugh.

"Whatcha making?" he asks.

"Scarf for my daughter. I know, I know, a scarf is cliché for knitting. I'm just a beginner, though."

"Beginning knitter, huh," Moses says.

Butterflies.

He wants to say more. To ask more. To tell her everything.

There is something right about it. Something gingerly pushing them toward one another.

He is reminded that he is still alive, that even though his mind is often in another room (one that he sometimes forgets is a part of the house), his feelings are always right there. He's still embarrassed when he needs help in the bathroom, still frustrated when the woman with the guitar cancels her event, and still laughs with Roy at Poker Night. He hasn't lost his ability to feel. Including, it turns out, his ability to feel some kind of love.

Not Helen love. Something tugs at him and cements in his heart that there would never be another Helen. Hell, he thinks, I'll be better off when I let go and join her.

But right now, there's the marshmallow lady.

Since the morning in the multi-purpose room, it's Rose and Moses. Every day at breakfast. Lunch. Afternoons. Chatting. I sit with these two every time they talk. Authentic exchanges stand out in this city, especially compared to those along the Strip, where the liquor is flowing, the bass is bumping, and the decisions are clumsy.

Rose tells him about their seven cats. He tells her about the hummingbird that once made her nest in their backyard.

"By God, you've never seen a hummingbird so still, ever, unless she was sitting on her eggs. And did she sit there. Diligently. We'd sit outside and just watch her sit in that nest. Like a painting. A creature so naturally in motion being still for once."

"Never in my house," says Rose. "Nothing was ever still," she says. "Rushing, rushing, rushing. All over the place. My Bill died twenty years ago and I can still hear his clackety shoes."

Over the months that follow, Moses sleeps better. Finds his words more quickly. Onion soup is more flavorful.

Let's speed up to late September 2021. Multi-Purpose Room A.

"I think I might kind of love you, Rose Woods."

"No, no no," she says, shaking her head and smiling.

"Why no? Why can't I be in love?"

"We already had our turn," she says.

"But is it *turns*? Can't we just ...?"

"No. Love comes in a whole package. Part of the package is the future."

"Well, honey. We are the future. We're past the future. So what the heck do we have to lose?"

"No."

"Why?" he asks, taking her wrinkled hand in his coarse ones.

"Bill Woods was a good man," she says. "Never fell short on a promise. I held him while he died. He was my best friend. Since we were seventeen. It is a novel, an epic, our lives, too long and big and real to try to do it again."

"Rose," says Moses, laughing. "I don't want to marry you. I want to love you. And I want you to love me."

She studies him. The flower in her hair lets off a scent that reminds him of Helen's garden. And that humming-bird, and those tiny eggs, and that tiny beginning.

"I think I met you ... to make me better. And I want to hold onto that," he says.

"People hold on too tight to things. We have to release them."

"How, Rose? How do we release them? How do I let

Helen go?"

"I can't tell you how you will heal, Moses. Only me."

He lets go of her hand. Jams his thumb and forefinger into his eyes and wipes them clean.

Rose takes in a breath.

"I'm not trying to replace Bill," he says. "And you wouldn't be replacing Helen."

"Moses," she says, "rhymes with Roses."

"Can love just be this?" Moses asks. "Me and you at Atria Sutton. Just us, right now, Rose Woods? We don't even have to call it love. We can call it ... marshmallows."

She laces her fingers through his.

I keep my eye on Rose and Moses
Love is a nutrient
a vitamin
a muscle
and they are getting their exercise again
Love is
a dose of tenderness every day

Our second story takes place in Summerlin. It's August 2018. Meet Faye, 44 years old. A high school English teacher. Divorced for three years. She's been dating Kyle, the rugby guy. He's separated (but still married). He uses the word "hiatus" to describe why he lives in Las Vegas and his wife lives in San Francisco.

"So," Faye says, one evening over wine and pizza, "I have to ask you this question."

"Shoot," says Kyle. She shoots.

"When you said that you and your wife are 'on hiatus,' what does that exactly mean? I mean, what exactly are we doing here?"

Kyle seemed to answer all her questions honestly (well, as honestly as a man who's still married, but is dating another woman can be).

No, the wife didn't know that he was seeing Faye.

No, likely that she had no idea at all that he was even putting himself out there in this way.

No. It was not at all how Faye had perceived it when he'd said the word "hiatus" weeks ago.

That was the last night that she saw Kyle, rugby guy.

Then there was Stuart. They meet taking out their trash at the apartment complex.

"How are you?" she asks.

"Good, you?"

"Great. Nice night."

"It is a nice night for trash," he says.

"Right," she says.

"I always wait too long to take it out, though," he says, "and then I have to do the old shove-down with the foot. But not until I put my shoe on."

She laughs.

Somehow, the way that he shares weird details like that in such an unabashed way is charming. Her ex-husband, Ed, had been so proper and intellectual, which at first she had loved, but which became exhausting after 15 years.

"Well, I've got my shoes on, too," she says, the rhythm of her heartbeat carrying her forward, "because I'm going for a walk on the trail. Do you want to join me?"

Over the next few weeks, they walk, talk, have coffee. Start texting. He's divorced. Two years. Let's speed up to right now. Her apartment. Chinese takeout. He takes a call from his mom. Luckily, "Mom" is a very loud talker on the phone and Faye hears the words, "Did you tell her that we had sex last night?"

Her heart stings. Stuart stands up and mouths that he's going to take this outside.

Faye takes in a breath.

She sees herself, probably a year before her divorce was final.

Ed had been in the bedroom on the phone, taking a work call, while she was in the kitchen, cutting potatoes.

"I've got to get out of the house," he'd said. He was laughing under his breath. She strained to hear what was coming next.

"I need you to call me back in a few and make something up. You need me to come back to the office, yadda yadda, we have to wrap up." More laughing. The potatoes were now thicker than she wanted them to be. They wouldn't bake all the way through unless they were thin, but she was tired of slicing, and Ed was scheming, and her heart was breaking, fracturing. How could they stay together when he didn't even want to be together? This whole meal was *for* him. And it was the beginning of her summer vacation. They were supposed to kick it off together. Teaching high-school English is definitely her calling, but she will never deny the beauty of ten weeks off every summer.

Ed received that call, five minutes later, as planned. He'd been hugging her in the kitchen, telling her how good the chicken smelled. But darn, wouldn't you know it, he had to go back in to work, a case needed to be wrapped up, he'd thought he'd finished up for the day. Shoot. He was so sorry. She kissed him goodbye and swallowed down the mountain in her throat. Again. She ate chicken and under-cooked potatoes alone that night, finishing *Wintergirls* by Laurie Halse Anderson (definitely not a feel-good).

And she's back in the present. Stuart is about to slip out the front door and chat some more with "Mom."

"Oh my God," Faye blurts out, bolting from the

couch toward him. "Your mom? You and 'Mom' have a very interesting relationship, don't you?"

His eyes are wide, he's speechless, holding his phone up to his ear.

"Hey," Faye says, leaning into his cell, "you can have him. What a catch!"

"Okay, I can totally explain," he says, clicking his phone off.

"No, I think I'm done listening to your jacked-up explanations. Get out of my apartment," she says. He bends down to grab his shoes.

"Get out *now*," she says, opening the door and pushing him out into the hallway.

"My shoes!" he says.

"Shove your dumb trash down with your sock from now on, asshole. And never talk to me again," she says, slamming the door, his shoes still on her side of it.

The next morning, she finds out that Stuart *lives* with his ex. Yes! In the building across from her! Or who knows, she thinks, maybe he's even still married! That evening, she drops his Vans in the dumpster. She's crushed, but more than that, she's surprised that she actually pushed him out of her apartment.

But she isn't this person.

But she is.

But she's supposed to be this smart role model for

her students. Dating a married man whose wife lives in another state, then getting involved with a divorced man who lives with his ex-wife? Where is the Faye that she thought she was? Perhaps the correct question is: Why can't some men get their shit together? But that's another Vegas story for another time.

Faye is reinventing herself. Blowing up the essence of who she thinks she's supposed to be: someone who does everything right, checks things off the list, does what you're supposed to do. Avoids mistakes, because mistakes are bad.

I'm speeding up time now.

Faye starts hiking. With a girlfriend at first, then solo. She'd grown up downtown in the '80s and '90s, during the boom that brought in the Mirage, Excalibur, and Treasure Island. When Circus Circus built its candy-colored shell. She'd never experienced as a child what the city has to offer outside of all of that. She becomes a regular at the café and the library in Blue Diamond.

And during those long hikes, Faye starts to get that sensation that you get when you start regaining feeling in your leg or your arm after it falls asleep. It's like her whole soul has been asleep for so long, and now, at almost 45 years old, she's coming alive. It's during this time that she meets Henry.

The first thing she notices is that he's tall. And the

second is that he's alone, like her. Also, he's wearing a backpack, like her, and he's sipping water from his water-bladder nozzle. And like her, he's browsing the "Western Culture" section in the Blue Diamond Library on a Tuesday in July.

Who does that?

"Have you read any Stegner?" he asks her.

"I haven't, but he's on my list," she says. "I want to read the one that won the Pulitzer."

"I'm reading it now," he says. "*Angle of Repose*."

They stare at each other. She lets out a long sigh.

"Wow," she says.

Yes. Wow.

Henry and Faye spend an hour in the Blue Diamond Library playing Scrabble in the recreation room. Ed wasn't into board games and she'd always wished he were. Scrabble had always reminded her of her mother, a retired high school English teacher, knower of all literary references, her very best friend. In that hour, Henry wins Scrabble by a hair, he tells her about his divorce, and she tells him about hers, they make plans to hike the next day. And the next day turns into three years.

I visit these two regularly
grappling with their pasts
integrating their children

crossing fingers
rolling dice
regenerating
from dust and debris

There is one more story before I head back out, onto the breeze. Meet Maria, 18 years old. It's May 2021 and we're at her high school graduation party. Maria lives over on Lanai, off Sandhill and Charleston. Her large family is crammed into the backyard, mariachi blasting. Her dad, David, is roasting a pig on a spit, a family tradition since forever ago.

She and her best friend Kiley have snuck rum and lemonades into her room.

With a little bit of liquid courage, Maria starts.

"Just sit," she says to Kiley.

"What, bitch?" Kiley says, "I seriously need to run through that sprinkler."

"Just. Please," says Maria.

"'Kay." Kiley sits. Maria takes a breath.

"So," Maria says.

"Soooooo," says Kiley, looking around Maria's room. Tons of pictures of the two of them on the bulletin board. "Oh my God, you still have that?" She points to the keychain of the penny that they smashed at Death Valley, freshman year. "And oh my God!" Kiley sits up and rushes to Maria's desk. "This!" She holds up the Scrabble trophy that they won together at camp in fifth grade. "Mar! You keep *everything*. I guess we haven't hung in your room in ages. I love all this."

Kiley gets teary. Maria gets teary.

Okay, it's time.

"Yup," says Maria, flipping the non-shaved side of her hair out of her eye. "I keep everything that means something to me."

Kiley paws at the trophy. "I'm sure mine got lost in one of the moves."

"So listen," says Maria. She's rehearsed this. *If not now, when?* she'd asked herself last night.

"So, like, I just ..." she starts again. There's a huge lump in her throat.

She wants to say so much. These are feelings she's always had, in general, and now they are very specific, and they are very Kiley. She didn't know how hard it'd be to say them out loud. But she knows she has to. Somehow, there is a crescendo in her life right now, there is a build that's taking her with it and she will be dust if she doesn't at least speak.

"Ki," she says. "What I want to say ... is, well, I'm leaving for Boulder in the fall and you're off to Rutgers."

"Amen," says Kiley, sipping her cocktail. "Get me out of this city."

Maria nods. But she doesn't want to leave this city. She doesn't want to leave her family or her tiny pink house that's been her solid foundation her whole life. She doesn't want to leave Doug, her amazing French horn teacher for the past eight years who took this little Mexican girl on, acknowledged her potential and talent, welcomed her into the world of symphonies and composers. Mostly, she doesn't want to leave Kiley.

"Girl, you are gonna be a star in Boulder, Ms. Full-ride Music Scholarship."

"Right," says Maria. "Totally. But I will miss my second chair playing the thirds below me."

"I will not miss playing a low F. Ever. Again," says Kiley.

Both girls drink and giggle. Maria and Kiley have made up the horn section in the Las Vegas High School Jewel of the Desert Marching and Symphonic Bands for four years.

"You will not have time for low Fs because you will be changing the world of Psychology at Rutgers."

"And I'm minoring in Women's Studies. Did I tell you that?"

"Awesome," says Maria.

It's torture. Every. Single. Thing about Kiley drives her crazy. Just when she knows that it can't get any worse, Kiley does or says something else amazing. Again. Like dying her hair a new color. Or telling off a douchey guy at school. Or correcting a teacher with the actual correct information (politely). And it all piles on top of Maria's heart and she knows that if she doesn't open up and say something, she will be smothered and she will just die.

"Okay, bitch, what did you want to tell me? It's hot and I need sprinklers."

Maria takes a deep breath.

Yes. Now.

"Well. What I wanted to tell you is about ... love."

Kiley freezes. Grasps the Scrabble trophy a little tighter.

"What I want to tell you is that ... I've loved you since fifth grade."

Kiley's mouth is open, and her heart is melting.

"Since you told me that you hid in the closet at after-school and read Roald Dahl books because all the after-school kids sucked and made fun of your eye patch. Since you told me how you stood in another closet once, your mom's, and watched while her husband punched her. You were eight. Since you told me how your youngest brother didn't speak until he was four."

The longer the words tumble out, the more solid Maria's voice sounds, like the way her horn tone has become richer and more refined over the eight years that she's been playing.

"I loved you when you challenged me for first chair

and you lost and you were mad at me for that one day."

Kiley smiles. Nods. Wipes her eyes.

"I loved you when you spent the night over spring break because Andy moved in and you didn't like him and you were trying to prove a point to your mom. I love your eff-you attitude, how you always speak up, how comfortable you are in any situation. I've loved you for a long, long time, and if I don't tell you about it right now, when we're both about to leave for college, I feel like I'll just break into a million pieces. And so. There."

Kiley opens her mouth wider and nothing comes out. She bursts into tears.

Finally, Kiley speaks. "I ... I don't know how to ... those are the nicest things anyone has ever said to me, probably will ever say to me."

Maria doesn't want Kiley to think she's nice. She doesn't want to be a memory of nice things once said, and that's that.

"I wish ..." says Kiley. She bites her lip, unable to meet Maria's eyes.

Maria shakes her head. "As my dad says, 'If you wish in one hand and take a shit in the other, guess which one fills up faster?'"

They giggle. Then there's silence. Heavy silence that's full of the hints Maria's left for Kiley all year. Their prom picture. The night they actually cuddled. A kiss on the cheek. But Maria has known all along that Kiley is not into it like *that*, not just not into *Maria*. It's always been hard for Maria, having "girlfriends." But now that the weight has been lifted from her chest, the words are out of her head and her heart, Maria feels like a chord resolved. She's surprised that she's not crying.

"Hey," says Maria. "There is one thing that would be cool right now."

"What?" asks Kiley.

"Bipperies!"

"Yes, bitch!"

The girls unbuckle their horn cases, which happen to be right here in Maria's room, because they just played at graduation. They spend the next hour playing duets loudly, intermittently sipping lemonade, while their families party in the backyard.

With her horn resting on her thigh, the taste of nickel (and rum) on her lips, and schmaltz flowing from her fingers, Maria wants these moments to stretch into forever: harmonizing with her best friend and sharing this thing that they both love. Saying farewell to their child-selves.

What drew Maria to the horn when she was in 7th grade was its shape. The curves and the valves and the majesty of the instrument. The mystery of all of that tubing, and how sound travels through it to come out of the bell. As they finish up Bipperie No. 4, Maria thinks about

how there is mystery ahead for both of them, how they
are about to travel to unknown parts of their lives where
there is music yet to be played.

Well.
I can't see too far past Sunrise Mountain
all the way to Boulder and New Brunswick
but Maria brings a young woman
home for Christmas her sophomore year
and Kiley stays just Kiley
graduating from Rutgers with honors
visiting Las Vegas every few years or so
and makes a plan with Maria
every single visit
some years, they get out their horns

One more
quick
zig-zag in time
before I float off

Back to Moses and that hummingbird
the stillness
after the
frenzy
of

buzzing
wings

Take a minute
if you can
to pause
and breathe deep
creosote and pine
Joshua trees
and pink hedgehog cactus flowers

This is for
you
who live here
the cogs and the wheels
the roots

We're more than the volcano,
than the rooftop pools,
than the buffets and the residencies
more than what they see
when the pilot lowers the landing gear

We're the dirt underneath Cactus Joe's
we're finding love in nursing homes
we're evolving, becoming more whole for our stu-

dents
    we're graduates, returning home from college to give back

    We plant seeds
    grow
    we implode
    we reinvent
    we regenerate
    prayers sent up

    love
    every day
       in Las Vegas

Contributors

Emily Bordelove is currently working on her MFA in Popular Fiction Writing and Publishing at Emerson College. She published dozens of articles with *Odyssey Online* during her undergraduate career, and performed a reading of her gothic short story "Home Sweet Home" at an event (and a limited-edition chapbook anthology) titled *Scary Stories From Around the World*. When she's not cuddled up on the couch with a book and a cup of tea, she can be found cheering on her local hockey teams the Vegas Golden Knights and the Henderson Silver Knights.

Photo by Josh Hawkins

Melissa Bowles-Terry is a tenured member of the library faculty at the University of Nevada, Las Vegas. She previously worked at University of Wyoming Libraries, and earned a Master's degree in Library and Information Science at the University of Illinois, Urbana-Champaign. She is co-author of the book *Classroom Assessment Techniques for Librarians* (2015), published by the Association of College and Research Libraries. She grew up on the Idaho-Utah border on a farm that has been in her family for more than a century and has lived in Southern Nevada for seven years.

Bob Dancer is America's premier video poker writer and teacher. He has written ten books, including his best-selling autobiography *Million Dollar Video Poker* and the hyper-erotic *Sex, Lies, and Video Poker*. He is a co-host of a weekly podcast, *Gambling with an Edge*, and teaches two ten-week semesters of free video poker classes every year at the South Point. Contact him at bobdancerlasvegas@yahoo.com.

Kimberley Idol is a writer, writing instructor, and writing coach in Las Vegas. Partial to dogs, books, movies, good friends, and laughter, she is also an avid rock-climber and trekker and has spent much of her life traveling "rough": One backpack, one round-trip ticket in and out of the biggest airport in the area—that's all Kim needs. She has spent the last few years in the Middle East and in Asia, and she loves the wilderness and the outdoors. Her memoir *How Did I Get Here?*, about working in the elephant stables of Nepal, is available everywhere books are sold.

Jarret Keene is an Assistant Professor in the English Department at the University ot Nevada, Las Vegas, where he teaches American literature and the graphic novel. He has written books—travel guide, rock-band biography, poetry collections—and edited short-fiction anthologies such as *Las Vegas Noir* and *Dead Neon: Tales of Near-Future Las Vegas*.

Heather Lang-Cassera is Clark County, Nevada, Poet Laureate Emeritus (2019-2021) and was named Las Vegas' 2017 "Best Local Writer" by the readers of Nevada Public Radio's *Desert Companion*. Heather holds a master of Fine Arts in Creative Writing with a Certificate in Literary Translation from Fairleigh Dickinson University. She is a founder and Senior Editor at Tolsun Books, and is the World Literature editor with *The Literary Review*. She serves Nevada State College as a Lecturer teaching College Success and Creative Writing, and as a faculty advisor for the literary magazine *300 Days of Sun*. Heather's poetry chapbook, *I Was the Girl With the Moon-Shaped Face*, was published by Zeitgeist Press in 2018. She published her full-length collection, *Gathering Broken Light*, in 2021 with Unsolicited Press. The writing of *Gathering Broken Light* was supported in part by a Project Grant for Artists from the Nevada Arts Council. You can learn more about her at www.heatherlang.cassera.net.

Photo by Richard Malit

Nicole Minton is a writer and editor from California. Her paper "Gender Fluidity and the Unexplored Side of Hemingway" was presented at the Johns Hopkins Richard Macksey National Undergraduate Symposium in 2021. She is currently enrolled in an Advanced MA Track program in English with plans of pursuing a PhD. When she isn't studying, she can be found playing music, planning road trips, and walking her dog. This is her first published fiction.

Jen Nails is the K-12 Librarian at the Adelson Educational Campus in Las Vegas, and the author of the middle-grade novels *One Hundred Spaghetti Strings* (HarperCollins, 2017) and *Next to Mexico* (HMH, 2008). Her current work-in-progress novel centers on the fictional implosion of the STRAT Hotel, Casino & Skypod and features a trio of eighth graders growing up in Las Vegas who struggle to adapt to foundation-shaking changes in their lives while still holding onto the essence of who they really are. Jen's most cherished projects are her sons, Zac and Simon. You can learn more about her at www.jennails.com.

Photo by Mikayla Whitmore

Krystal Ramirez is an interdisciplinary artist working at the intersection of a second-generation immigrant background and growing up in a candy-colored, working-class landscape such as Las Vegas. With a particular interest in continuing conversations on materiality and experience to include aspects of race, gender, and more complex American experiences, she investigates the power of language and material over people, both intellectually and emotionally, and creates works that explore liminal spaces between destinations that aren't meant to exist in as much as passed through. By introducing instability to language and imagery, she creates a space to explore impermanence in areas we like to think of as stable and fixed. She is currently an MFA candidate in Art Practice at Stanford University.

Brett Riley is a writer and a professor of English at the College of Southern Nevada. He grew up in southeast Arkansas and spent his young adulthood in south Louisiana, where he earned his PhD at Louisiana State University. The father of three children, Riley is an animal lover who owns a dog and two cats. He has two granddaughters. Riley is the author of *The Subtle Dance of Impulse and Light* (Ink Brush Press), *Comanche* (Imbrifex Books), *Lord of Order* (Imbrifex Books), *Freaks* (2022), and *Travelers* (2022). He has published more than thirty short stories in journals such as *The Baltimore Review*, *f(r)iction*, *Solstice*, *Folio*, *The Evansville Review*, and many others. His nonfiction essays have appeared in *Role Reboot*, *Broad River Review*, *Rougarou*, *Green Hills Literary Lantern*, *Literary Orphans*, *Under the Gum Tree*, *Wild Violet*, and *Foliate Oak Magazine*. Follow Brett on Twitter and Instagram: @brettwrites.

Photo by Mikayla Whitmore

Nicholas Russell is a writer from Las Vegas. His writing has been featured in *The Believer, Defector, The Guardian, Reverse Shot, Mic, Columbia Journal,* and *The Point,* among other publications. He's a contributing prose editor at *Burrow Press Review* and a bookseller at the Writer's Block.

Author and actress **Tonya Todd** plunged into Las Vegas, the Entertainment Capital of the World, to immerse herself in bright lights, a big city, and even bigger dreams. As the Education Chair for Henderson Writers Group, she works at building a strong literary community that celebrates and embraces a variety of voices. Tonya is invested in "own voices" writing, and diverse representation in both the literary and cinematic worlds she inhabits. Her involvement in the literary, theatre, and filmmaking communities provides a platform to champion marginalized artists. In her role as host of the *The 52 Love Podcast*, she interviews a myriad of like-minded creatives dedicated to celebrating love and art in all its forms. To connect with Tonya, follow her social media (@MsTonyaTodd) and her IMDb page at imdb.me/TonyaTodd.

Mauricio Ortiz Zaragoza is a writer and scholar based in Las Vegas, the place he has called home for 20 years after immigrating from Querétaro City, Mexico. He has completed his bachelor's degree in Sociology with a minor in Film from the University of Nevada, Las Vegas. He is currently finishing up a graduate certificate in Social Justice Studies at UNLV while helping run the family business. His research interests include critical theory, film, video games, and gender and sexuality. He enjoys spending an inordinate amount of his income on vinyl records and CriterionCollection releases. He also shoots film photography.

About Huntington Press

Huntington Press is a specialty publisher of Las Vegas- and gambling-related books and periodicals, including the award-winning consumer newsletter, *Anthony Curtis' Las Vegas Advisor.*

Huntington Press
3665 Procyon Street
Las Vegas, Nevada 89103
LasVegasAdvisor.com
e-mail: books@huntingtonpress.com

A Change is Gonna Come

The stories, essays, and — for the first time — poetry in *A Change Is Gonna Come* explore this rich concept in ways large and small.

A Valley of Light and Shadow

This 11th volume of the annual Las Vegas Writes anthology, *A Valley of Light and Shadow* walks the thin neon line between salvation and damnation.

Anarchy of Memories

These stories from eight of Las Vegas' most creative writers place Las Vegas celebrities in imaginative settings and intriguing circumstances.

Back to Where You Once Belonged

This eighth volume in the Las Vegas Writes series joins the timeless with the personal when it comes to negotiating the passage between then and now.

Getting Better All the Time

Progress is a motive force in every city—and, perhaps, the point of civilization itself. In these stories and essays by some of Las Vegas' finest writers, you will see how locals weave spectacle, risk, and reward into the narratives of civic, political, financial, personal, and spiritual progress ... or, sometimes, calamity.

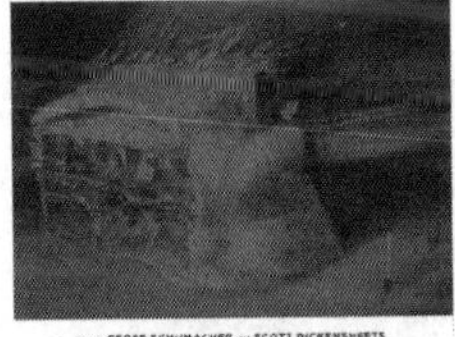

Live Through This

Las Vegas was built on millions of intimate unnatural disasters, such as bad turns of the cards or unlucky rolls of the dice. In both fiction and essays, this anthology extends the dynamic of unnatural disaster beyond the gambling parlors and into the streets, homes, and and eccentric spaces of Las Vegas.

Lost and Found in Las Vegas

The central concept of a "lost-and-found" box and the random and disparate items that might be found within is the perfect metaphor for Las Vegas, a metropolis with such singular energies, generated by the juxtaposition—and sometimes collision—of so many diverse and frenetic elements. In no other city is it so easy to get lost, nor so vital to be found.

Visit
LasVegasAdvisor.com
for all the latest on
gambling and Las Vegas

Become a *Las Vegas Advisor* Member and get our exclusive coupons and members-only discounts.

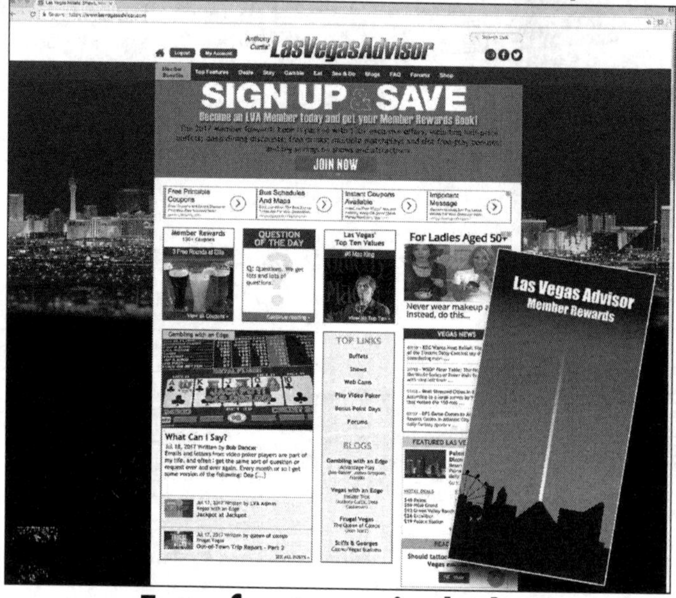

Free features include:

- Articles and ongoing updates on gambling.

- Tournament listings and articles.

- Up-to-the-minute Las Vegas gambling promotion announcements.

- Question of the Day—In-depth answers to gambling and Las Vegas related queries.

- Active message boards with discussions on blackjack, sports betting, poker, and more!